瑞蘭國際

瑞蘭國際

搭配詞的力量
THE POWER OF COLLOCATIONS

名詞篇

全新升級版

序

　　對於很多台灣的大學畢業生而言，畢業後「不務正業」做一些和主修八竿子打不著的工作已成為一個普遍的現象。而我能將我的大學、研究所所學，緊緊地和我的工作——英語教學——緊扣著，用著這樣的「幸運」好好做些什麼事，是我一直感激的。

　　2011 年 9 月，受到 Pit Corder 一篇 1967 年的經典文章〈The Significance of Learner Errors〉當中所述，對於了解「怎麼學」要在了解「怎麼教」之前之必要性所啟發，我毅然決然從賓州大學離開至哥倫比亞大學教育生研究院，在那開啟了對於第二語言習得（Second language acquisition）的深度學習。

　　在學習過程中，影響我特別深的，是一位叫韓照紅（ZhaoHong Han）的中國籍女教授。認識她的人，包括很多學界的教授，都知道她講話鏗鏘有力，授課風格極為嚴格且犀利。讓對知識有真熱情的學生，修習她的課程如入寶山。

　　對於精通中文、英文、日文，也曾經粗淺地學習過法文的我，她曾經跟我談到，因為我有眾多學習語言的經驗，我會有更多更準確的「直覺」（stronger intuitions），知道可能什麼才是較正確的學習語言方法，而我們可以再去用實證研究去驗證那些直覺。也就是在研究第二語言習得的過程當中，認知到了「chunking-based learning」（語塊學習）的重要性。

眾多認知心理學研究顯示，我們的大腦，相對於「離散」（discrete）的資訊，對於記憶一塊有連結性、有系統的資訊群比較在行。而「collocations」（搭配詞）的學習，即是因應大腦這樣的特性。同時也可以讓我們在思考字和字如何搭配使用時，防堵我們的「中文想法」或「中文概念」滲透進去。搭配詞就是一個詞組，而這個詞組裡頭可能包含兩個甚至兩個以上習慣搭配在一起的字（A collocation is a familiar grouping of words, especially words that habitually appear together.）。由於每個語言都有它們習慣組合字詞的方式，所以熟稔搭配詞對於幫助我們正確且道地地使用語言，會有極大的幫助。

　　例如，我們中文可以說「學習新知」，但是「learn new knowledge」卻是錯誤的英文。例如，當我們要表達「確切的日期」時，英語母語人士能夠直覺地、不假思索地使用出來「a firm date」，這也是搭配詞的力量。更不用說英文母語人士公式般地（所以也有人稱搭配詞為 formulaic expression），使用出「gain a deeper understanding of sth」（對於～有更深入地了解），這也是搭配詞所互相結合的產物。

　　但相對於學習者，英語母語人士在習得搭配詞的過程是一個較自然、不費力的過程，甚至有可能不自覺。但對於第二外語學習者來說（成人尤是），由於先天後天條件和學習環境都較不利，需要有一個管道，能接觸到眾多的搭配詞。

因為這樣的一個契機，我從 2015 年起辦了超過 100 場搭配詞學習免費公開課、也在 2016 年創建了「搭配詞的力量」Facebook 專頁，同時也撰寫了《搭配詞的力量 Collocations：名詞篇》這一本書。本書結集了眾知名搭配詞字典（Macmillan Collocations Dictionary, Oxford Collocations Dictionary, BBI Combinatory Dictionary of English, Longman Collocations Dictionary and Thesaurus）和種種語料庫，整理出來台灣人最需要的搭配詞、以及沒有記憶的話，極容易受到「中文腦」影響而用錯的搭配詞。目前市面上的搭配詞用書，大多是厚重的字典，沒有中文翻譯輔助，有時也過度繁雜，比較像是工具書，其實不太適合學習者直接學習。

　　「搭配詞的力量」一系列書，希望站在巨人的肩膀上，能夠提供對搭配詞學習有興趣的台灣學習者，最直接的幫助。希望本書能作為學習者一個新的立基點，從今以後能讓「語塊學習」、「搭配詞」等等的新觀點，有效提升英語能力，不再「字字是英文，句句非英文」，「年年學英文，年年從頭學」。

創勝文教共同創辦人

王梓沅

2019 年 3 月

搭配詞如何給你力量？
為何搭配詞那麼重要呢？

到底什麼是「搭配詞」（collocations）呢？
定義上來看，搭配詞組就是每個語言約定俗成上的字詞搭配
方式。而那些特別高頻的搭配詞組，即泛稱為搭配詞。

★ 你是否有想要講一句話，但是語塞講不出來，因為「不知道要用
什麼字表達心中所想的東西」的經驗呢？
★ 你是否有時會覺得自己的英文看似「字字是英文」，但其實「句
句不是英文」，不知如何道地、精準地使用英文呢？
★ 你是否知道的單字不少，但是真的用出來的總是那些呢？

如果你曾經有以上的感覺過，那麼很可能代表你的英文搭配詞
記得不夠多喔！母語人士之所以講話能如此精準、流利，其中一個
原因來自於他們頭腦中有眾多的搭配詞，幫助他們有效率、精準地
表達想法。若我們用中文習慣的方式去思考字與字的組合，就很容
易造成很多的「台式英文」（Chinglish）。其實很多搭配習慣，是
沒有什麼原因的。我們直接來看看以下幾個字組。

對中文母語人士來說，我們會不假思索地講出「吃藥」。但對
英美人士來講，「eat medicine」卻是個錯誤的表達方式（英文：
take medicine）。而你知道嗎？在日文裡頭，他們的藥是用喝的喔
（薬を飲む）！

這樣的差異，其實在語言中，屢見不鮮。例如，我們再來看看中文、英文在祝賀人生日時的差異。

對於中文母語人士來說，「生日快樂」是我們會不假思索使用的。但你有注意到嗎？對我們的「中文耳」而言，「Happy Birthday」（生日開心）這樣的賀詞，是較不通順的。但 Happy 這個字，「開心」跟「快樂」都是合理的翻譯時，我們的「中文腦」要如何去做選擇呢？而日本人卻是用「生日恭喜」（お誕生日おめでとう）呢！

《搭配詞的力量 Collocations：名詞篇》一書，即因應台灣人學習英語的需求而生。作者從語料庫中整理出英語學習者頻繁使用的名詞，並列出和其搭配使用的動詞、形容詞、以及慣用法等，並精選例句輔以學習，希望能夠加深大家對這些高頻名詞的認識。

例如，就「effort」這個字而言，不少人知道是「努力」的意思。但在「effort」一章節當中，本書就介紹了「last-ditch effort」這樣的用法，也就是「最後一躍」的意思喔！而像在「expectation」一章節中，我們介紹了像是「live up to one's expectations」（符合某人的期待）如此的用法，讓我們對於「expectation」的認識，從知道是「期待」，能夠進一步知道如何使用這個字。

Effort 努力，努力的成果 ▶ MP3-055

Adj. + effort

all-out / concentrated / considerable / enormous / huge / massive / strenuous / tremendous effort	極大的努力
brave / heroic / valiant effort	勇敢的努力
painstaking effort	苦功、心血
desperate / frantic effort	拚命的、瘋狂的努力
final / last / last-ditch effort	最後的努力
continuing / ongoing / sustained effort	持續的努力
feeble / half-hearted effort	少許的努力
fruitless / futile / vain effort	空忙、徒勞無功
worthwhile effort	值得的努力
grass-roots effort	基層的努力
concerted / joint effort	共同的努力
get-out-the-vote effort	為催票所做的努力

73

V. + expectation

have / hold expectations	有～期待、期望
beat / exceed / go beyond / outperform / surpass expectations	超乎預期（好）
come up to / fit in with / fulfill / live up to / match / meet / satisfy expectations	達到期望、符合預期
dampen / dash / disappoint / fall short of expectations	期望破滅（= 不如預期）
confound / contradict / defy / shatter / violate expectations	期望落空、不符預期

補充 注意和 confound 後面可以接 expectations， confound 後面也常接版 predictions（與情感不同）

heighten / raise expectations	提高期望
lower expectations	降低期望
build / create / set expectations	造成期待、建立期望

expectation + V.

expectations grow / rise	期望升高
expectations change	期望改變

84

一個語言要學好，一定要用對方法。希望這本書所載錄的搭配詞，能帶給大家在學習英文上，滿滿的力量。Happy learning.

創勝文教共同創辦人

王梓沅

2017 年 3 月

7

目次

R

S

T

U

Assistance 援助

Adj. + assistance

direct / emergency assistance	直接、緊急援助
mutual assistance	互助、相互協助
social / welfare assistance	社會、福利救助
humanitarian assistance	人道救援

V. + assistance

lend / provide / render assistance	給予協助
obtain / receive assistance	獲得協助
ask for / call for / seek assistance	尋求協助
turn to sb for assistance	向某人求助
be of / come to sb's assistance	幫助某人

例句❶ Japan is giving <u>social assistance</u> to "non regular" workers, a group that has long been ignored.

日本正在提供社會救助給一群長期被忽視的「非固定」勞動者。

例句❷ The government is willing to <u>lend assistance</u> to the victims of Typhoon Morakot.

政府願意提供協助給莫拉克風災的受災戶。

例句❸ I wish I had had someone to <u>turn to for assistance</u> when I was puzzled at that time.

我真希望當時有人可以幫助迷惘的我。

例句❹ Do let us know if we can <u>be of any assistance</u> to you.

如果我們可以幫上忙，麻煩你告訴我們。

Belief 信念、看法

Adj. + belief

firm belief	堅定的信念
unshakable / unwavering belief	不可動搖的信念
widely-held belief	普遍看法
long-standing belief	長期存在的看法
conflicting belief	互相矛盾的看法
misguided belief	錯誤的看法
deep-seated / deeply-held / deeply-ingrained belief	根深蒂固的看法

V. + belief

hold belief	抱持信念
adhere to / cling to / stick to belief	堅持信念
renounce belief	放棄信念
challenge / question / shake / undermine belief	動搖信念

belief + V.

belief persist	信念堅持、持續

例句 ① Contrary to widely-held belief, there is no real link between Australia and New Zealand.

澳洲和紐西蘭實際上並沒有相連，這與大眾普遍的想法恰恰相反。

例句 ② If rich economies raise import barriers in the misguided belief that they will protect Western living standards, they could be wrong.

如果富裕國家以為可以透過提高關稅壁壘來維護西方的生活水平，那就錯了。

例句 ③ The latest findings challenge a common belief that coffee is bad for people's health.

最新的研究結果質疑「咖啡有害健康」的普遍看法。

例句 ④ People's belief in the magical properties of this herb persisted down the centuries.

數百年來，民眾一直相信這藥草的神奇特性。

例句 ⑤ I am firmly of the belief that we need to improve our product.

我認為我們需要改良產品。

例句 ⑥ To the best of my belief, the information given in the application is correct.

據我所知，這份申請書上的資料是對的。

實用短語 / 用法 / 句型

• be of the belief that... 認為～

• to the best of one's belief 就某人所知道的
(= to the best of one's knowledge)

• a set of beliefs 一套信念（a set of 也常搭配 values 或 criteria）

• contrary to popular belief 和普遍看法相反的是

• beyond belief 難以置信

Blame 責任

V. + blame

shoulder / take blame	承擔責任
attach / attribute blame (+ to)	指責
lay / pin / place / put blame (+ on)	指責
pass / shift blame (+ onto)	推卸責任
absolve sb from / of blame	免除責任

Blame + V.

blame fall on / lie with / rest with sb	責任歸咎於～

補充 相似的用法：< responsibility fall on /
lie with / rest with sb > （責任歸咎於～）

例句❶ The company refused to <u>shoulder</u> any <u>blame</u> for the damage.

這間公司拒絕為損害負任何的責任。

例句❷ Unwilling to <u>place blame on</u> management, the manager pointed the finger at the employee for turning in the project late.

經理不願意將責任歸咎於管理上的問題，而是將矛頭指向了員工遲交計畫。

例句❸ We are all confused about why he could be <u>absolved of all blame</u>.

我們都很疑惑，為什麼他可以被免除所有的過失。

例句❹ Don't <u>lay the blame at my door</u>. You spilled food on the carpet, too!

不要只責怪我。你也把食物打翻在地毯上啊！

例句❺ The manager said he would take <u>a share of the blame for</u> the loss.

經理表示他會為公司的損失負責。

實用短語 / 用法 / 句型

• lay the blame at one's door 怪罪於某人

• part of / a share of the blame 部分責任

Competition 競爭

▶ MP3-007

Adj. + competition

cut-throat / formidable / intense competition	激烈的競爭
head-to-head competition	直接的競爭
domestic / local competition	國內競爭
global / international / overseas competition	海外競爭

V + competition

be up against competition	面臨競爭
go into competition	投入競爭
beat off / fight off / see off competition	擊敗競爭、脫穎而出
stifle competition	抑制競爭
be disqualified from / be eliminated from / be knocked out from competition	從競爭中被淘汰

competition + V.

competition heat up / intensify	競爭加劇

例句❶ We face <u>formidable competition</u> in every aspect of our business, particularly from companies that seek to connect people with information on the web and provide them with relevant advertising.

我們業務的每一方面都面臨著強大的競爭,這些競爭特別是來自於那些把網路資訊與人做聯繫,並提供相關廣告的公司。

例句❷ These days, we have <u>head-to-head competition</u> between companies where people do have patents.

近日來,我們面臨那些擁有專利權的公司的直接競爭。

例句❸ For economists, monopoly is never good for the market because it <u>stifles competition</u>.

經濟學家認為壟斷行為對市場不好,因為它會抑制競爭。

例句❹ The gas companies are having to lay off staff <u>in the face of stiff competition</u> from oil.

面對石油市場強烈的競爭,天然氣公司不得不解雇員工。

實用短語 / 用法 / 句型

• in competition with 與～競爭

• in the face of competition 面對競爭

Complaint 抱怨、控訴

Adj. + complaint

legitimate / valid / well-founded complaint	合理的抱怨
minor complaint	不重要的抱怨

V. + complaint

make / voice a complaint	抱怨
file / lodge / register a complaint	提出控告
dismiss / reject a complaint	駁回訴訟

▶ MP3-010

例句❶ The worker decided to file a complaint against her boss because of his sex discrimination.
因為老闆的性別歧視,這工人決定對老闆提出控告。

例句❷ The TV station has received a barrage of complaints about the amount of violence in the series.
因為影集中有太多的暴力畫面,電視台已經收到了一連串的投訴。

補充 a barrage of 後面也常搭配 questions(一連串的問題)、criticisms(一連串的批評)、protests(一連串的抗議)等。

例句❸ The company has received over 1,000 letters of complaints due to its low-quality products.
因為他們產品品質低劣,這公司已經收到超過 1,000 封的抱怨信。

例句❹ The way I was treated gave me no cause for complaint.
他們對待我的方式讓我沒有理由可以抱怨。

實用短語 / 用法 / 句型

- a chorus of complaint 齊聲抱怨
- a barrage of complaints 一連串的抱怨
- a letter of complaint 抱怨信
- cause for / grounds for complaint 抱怨的理由

Conclusion 結論

Adj. + conclusion

inescapable / inevitable conclusion	不可避免的結論
obvious / definite / firm conclusion	明確的結論
erroneous conclusion	錯誤的結論
hasty conclusion	匆促的結論
preliminary / tentative conclusion	初步的結論

V. + conclusion

arrive at / come to / draw / reach a conclusion	下結論
jump to / leap to a conclusion	妄下定論、冒然斷定
bring to / lead to / point to a conclusion	得到結論
reinforce / substantiate / support a conclusion	支持結論
confirm a conclusion	證實結論

▶ MP3-012

例句① In the end, we <u>came to the conclusion</u> that it would be quicker to go by train.

我們最後得到的結論是搭火車比較快。

例句② Don't <u>jump to conclusions</u>. We have to figure it out first.

不要妄下定論，我們應該先把事情搞清楚。

例句③ The data he collected <u>substantiated the conclusion</u> that too much caffeine is bad for people's health.

他蒐集的資料證實了過量的咖啡因有害人體健康的結論。

Confidence 自信、信心、信任 ▸ MP3-013

Adj. + confidence

great / supreme / tremendous / utter confidence	極大的信心
unshakable / unwavering confidence	不可動搖的信心
renewed confidence	重拾的自信、信心
new-found confidence	新獲得、新建立的信心
growing / increased confidence	漸增的信心
absolute / complete / full confidence	完全的信任

V. + confidence

acquire / gain confidence	獲得自信、信心
win (one's) confidence	博得（某人的）信任
bolster / boost / build (up) / improve confidence	提升自信、信心
instill confidence (+ in)	灌輸信心
breed / engender / generate confidence (+ in)	建立信心、信任
get back / rebuild / restore confidence	重拾自信、信心
exude / ooze / radiate confidence	流露、散發自信
lose confidence	失去信心
dent / erode / shake / undermine confidence	削弱、動搖信心

destroy / shatter confidence 摧毀、打擊信心

Confidence + V.

confidence decline / wane 信心衰減

confidence rise / soar 信心提升、大增

confidence drain (away) / evaporate / go 信心喪失

▶ MP3-014

例句❶ They seemed to have <u>unshakable confidence</u>; but when I got to know them better, they were overwhelmed with insecurity.

他們看似有不可動搖的信心，但當我更瞭解他們之後發現，他們心中充滿了不安。

例句❷ Palestinian officials complained that these Israeli measures undermined their ability to <u>win people's confidence</u> and restore law and order.

巴勒斯坦官員抱怨說，以色列的做法削弱了他們贏得民心並恢復法律秩序的能力。

例句❸ A key to a successful public speech is that your body language should <u>exude confidence</u>.

一場成功演講的關鍵在於，你的肢體語言要能展露自信。

例句❹ As the European debt crisis worsens and continues to <u>erode confidence</u> in the global economy, the region's headache is most likely to dominate the summit.

隨著歐債危機惡化並持續動搖人們對全球經濟的信心，該地區的頭痛事很有可能成為這次高峰會的焦點。

例句⑤ My <u>confidence drained</u> completely after my first major defeat.

第一次的重大挫敗後，我的信心一掃而空。

例句⑥ True <u>self-confidence</u> is constant and won't <u>evaporate</u>.

真正的自信是持續的，而且不會喪失。

實用短語 / 用法 / 句型

- a crisis of confidence 信任危機

- a lack of confidence 缺乏信心

Confusion 混亂、混淆、困惑

▶ MP3-015

Adj. + confusion

utter confusion	徹底的、全面的混亂
considerable confusion	相當大的困惑
mental confusion	精神、思想混亂

V. + confusion

sow / stir confusion	造成混亂、困惑
add to confusion	增加混亂、困惑
clarify / clear up / dispel confusion	排除混亂、澄清困惑
throw sb / sth into confusion	造成～混亂、困惑

confusion + V.

confusion arise / reign	產生混亂、困惑
confusion surround sth	困惑圍繞在～

補充 相似的用法：< controversy surround sth >
爭議圍繞在～

例句❶ The new policy made by the government <u>stirred</u> <u>confusion</u> among the citizens.

政府做的新決策讓市民感到相當困惑。

例句❷ Apple's latest decision has only <u>added to</u> the general confusion.

蘋果公司最新的決策徒增大眾的困惑。

例句❸ They picked off the officers first so as to <u>throw</u> the enemy troops <u>into confusion</u>.

他們先把軍官一個個擊斃,目的是使敵軍陷入混亂。

例句❹ I am concerned that doubts and <u>confusion</u> will <u>arise</u> in the study and transmission of his teaching.

我擔心的是,在研讀並傳授他教導的東西時會產生懷疑和混淆。

例句❺ When she opened the door, she was greeted by <u>a scene of</u> utter <u>confusion</u>.

她一開門就看見一片混亂不堪的景象。

實用短語 / 用法 / 句型

• a scene / state of confusion 混亂的場面

Consensus 一致、共識

▶ MP3-017

Adj. + consensus

general / prevailing consensus	廣泛的共識
unanimous consensus	一致的共識、一致同意
emerging / growing consensus	逐漸達成的、新興的共識
tacit / unspoken consensus	不言而喻的共識
scholarly consensus	學者的共識

V. + consensus

achieve / arrive at / come to / reach consensus	達成、取得共識
build / develop / forge consensus	建立、形成共識
call for / seek consensus	尋求共識
break / shatter consensus	打破共識

consensus + V.

consensus exist	共識存在
consensus break down	共識瓦解

例句❶ The talks achieved <u>general consensus</u> and positive results.

會談取得了大致的共識和正面的成果。

例句❷ Negotiations to finalize the agenda of the summit failed to <u>reach consensus</u> on any major initiatives.

確認高峰會議程的協商未能取得活動安排上的共識。

例句❸ They were in danger of <u>breaking</u> the political <u>consensus</u> that had been developed over the years.

他們面臨著可能會打破已經建立多年的政治共識的困境。

Contract 合約、契約

▶ MP3-019

Adj. + contract

formal / written contract	書面合約
verbal contract	口頭合約
valid contract	有效契約
void contract	無效契約
fat / lucrative contract	肥約、有利可圖的合約
binding contract	有約束力的合約
marriage contract	婚約
sweetheart contract	私底下簽訂的不法合約（美）

V. + contract

bid for / tender for a contract	投標爭取合約
award sb a contract / award a contract to sb	授與某人、簽訂合約以利～
secure / win a contract	獲得合約
draft / draw up a contract	擬訂合約
conclude / enter into / sign a contract	簽訂合約
carry out / execute / fulfill / honor a contract	履行合約
rescind / terminate a contract	終止合約
breach / violate a contract	違反合約

contract + V.

contract expire   合約到期

▶ MP3-020

例句❶ My advertising firm just won a fat contract with a cigarette company.
我的廣告公司剛和香菸公司簽了一份肥約。

例句❷ They awarded the construction contract to a French company.
他們將建設合約給了一家法國公司。

例句❸ In international trade, both the exporter and importer face risks as there is always the possibility that the other party may fail to fulfill the contract.
在國際貿易中，進出口雙方都面臨著風險，因為總存在對方不履行合約的可能性。

例句❹ If they don't get the test version of the software to us by tomorrow they'll be in breach of contract.
如果他們明天還不將軟體的測試版交給我們，他們就違約了。

例句❺ The underworld put out a contract on the prosecution witness.
黑社會雇人謀殺原告的證人。

實用短語 / 用法 / 句型

• be in breach of contract 違約

• put out a contract on sb 雇人謀殺、企圖謀害某人

Contrast 對比、對照

▶ MP3-021

Adj. + contrast

marked / sharp / stark / striking / strong contrast	明顯的、強烈的對比
startling contrast	驚人的對比
vivid / refreshing contrast	鮮明的對比

V. + contrast

make / offer / present / provide / show a contrast (+ to)	形成對比
draw / make a contrast (+ between / with)	與～做對比
heighten a contrast	提高、增加對比

▶ MP3-022

例句 ❶ Young and glamorous, she was a <u>refreshing contrast</u> to the male-dominated political establishment.
年輕有魅力的她與男性主導的政界形成鮮明的對比。

例句 ❷ The white walls <u>present a contrast</u> to the black carpet.
白牆和黑地毯形成對比。

例句 ❸ Their attitudes toward marriage stand in <u>stark contrast</u> to those of their parents.
他們對婚姻的看法和父母對婚姻的看法完全不同。

實用短語 / 用法 / 句型

• stand in contrast to sb / sth 和～完全不同

Controversy 爭論、爭議

Adj. + controversy

considerable / great controversy	相當大的爭議
bitter / fierce / heated / raging controversy	激烈的爭論

補充 heated 後面也常搭配 words（激烈的言詞）、
remarks（激烈的話語）、debate（激辯）

current controversy	目前的爭議
long-standing / ongoing controversy	持續不斷的爭議

V. + controversy

arouse / court / create / generate / give rise to controversy	引起爭議

補充 court（vt.）作及物動詞時有吸引、招致的意思，
如以下用法：< court disasters > 招致、導致災難，
< court talents > 吸引人才

fuel / provoke / spark (off) / stir up / trigger controversy	引發爭議
be dogged by / be surrounded by controversy	受爭議困擾、備受爭議
shy away from controversy	避開爭議
end / quell / resolve / settle controversy	平息、解決爭議
run into controversy	遭受質疑、備受爭議

controversy + V.

controversy arise / break out / erupt	產生、出現爭議
controversy rage / persist	爭議持續
controversy center on sth	爭議集中於某事
controversy surround sth	爭議圍繞在～

▶ MP3-024

例句❶ The relationship between financial openness and economic growth remains the subject of heated controversy.
金融開放與經濟成長的關係仍是極受爭議的話題。

例句❷ This year's NBA champion is dogged by controversy.
今年 NBA 的冠軍備受爭議。

例句❸ The network ran into controversy over claims of the documentary footage.
這個電視公司因為紀錄片片段的所有權問題備受爭議。

例句❹ Controversy is raging over the route of the new road.
新公路路線的爭議持續不斷。

例句❺ The proposal has stirred up a storm of controversy.
這個提案已經引發了極大的爭議。

實用短語 / 用法 / 句型

• be no stranger to controversy 對爭議司空見慣

• a firestorm / storm of controversy 極大的爭議

37

Cost 費用、成本、代價

Adj. + cost

considerable / enormous / prohibitive cost	龐大的費用、巨額成本
escalating / soaring / spiraling cost	高漲的費用、成本
hidden cost	隱藏成本
gross / net cost	淨成本
budgeted / projected cost	預計費用、成本
marginal cost	邊際成本
upfront cost	預付的費用
out-of-pocket cost	實際費用、成本
overhead cost	間接成本、固定成本
considerable / enormous / huge cost	龐大、重大的代價

V. + cost

cover / meet / pay cost	承擔、支付費用
bump up / drive up / push up cost	提高費用、成本
bring down / cut / drive down / slash cost	降低費用、成本
reimburse cost	償還費用
recoup / recover cost	補貼、彌補成本
defray cost	支付費用

| offset cost | 抵消費用、成本 |
| outweigh cost | 超過成本 |

cost + V.

| cost escalate / go up / shoot up / soar | 費用、成本增加 |
| cost fall / go down | 費用、成本減少 |

▶ MP3-026

例句❶ The <u>prohibitive cost</u> of lifting thousands of tons of equipment into space makes it uneconomical.
運送好幾千噸重的裝備到太空所費不貲，這使得整個計畫很不划算。

例句❷ The <u>spiraling cost</u> of gas and electricity combined with the impact of green taxes is putting people's health and lives at risk.
天然氣和電力的成本不斷上漲，再加上環保稅的影響，將危及民眾的健康與生命。

例句❸ Most of them took part-time jobs to help <u>defray the cost</u> of living in the U.S.
他們大部分的人都曾經打工賺錢來支付在美國的生活開銷。

例句❹ The company's <u>costs</u> have <u>shot up</u> over the last five years.
該公司的花費在過去五年內巨幅增加。

例句❺ We should promote the project <u>at all costs</u>.
我們無論如何都要推動這項計畫。

實用短語 / 用法 / 句型

• at a cost of~ 花費～元、以～為代價

• at all costs 不惜任何代價

Courage 勇氣

▶ MP3-027

Adj. + courage

immense courage	相當大的勇氣
extraordinary / remarkable courage	非凡、過人的勇氣
dauntless courage	無畏的勇氣

V. + courage

require / take courage	需要勇氣
demonstrate / display courage	展現勇氣
gather / muster (up) / pluck up / screw up / summon (up) courage	鼓起勇氣
admire / applaud one's courage	讚賞某人的勇氣

例句❶ A small team of Americans carried out the operation with immense courage and capability.

一支美國小隊以非凡的勇氣與能力完成了這次的行動。

例句❷ Being leaders, you have to overcome your pessimism and pluck up your courage to face the difficulties.

身為領導者，你必須克服悲觀的情緒並鼓起勇氣面對困難。

例句❸ When I think of his patience under adversity and his courage under fire, I am filled with an emotion of admiration I cannot put into words.

當我想起他在困境中的耐心以及在戰火中的勇氣，我心裡就充滿難以名狀的崇拜。

補充 < put~into words > 將～以言語形容

例句❹ John knew that Tom had started the fight, but he was afraid to say so; he did not have the courage of his convictions.

John 知道開頭打架的是 Tom，可是他不敢說，他沒有勇氣做自己認為對的事情。

實用短語 / 用法 / 句型

• courage under fire 戰火中的勇氣、生死豪情

• have the courage of one's convictions
勇於做自己認為對的事情、勇於～

• take courage and press on 勇於做自己認為對的事情、勇於～

• take one's courage in both hands 鼓起勇氣、勇往直前

Creativity 創意、創造力

▶ MP3-029

Adj. + creativity

collective creativity	集體創意

V. + creativity

demonstrate / express creativity	展現創意、創造力
develop creativity	發揮創意
inspire / spark / stimulate creativity	激發創意、創造力
foster / nurture creativity	培養創造力
enhance / promote creativity	提升創造力
inhibit / kill / stifle creativity	扼殺創意、創造力

▶ MP3-030

例句❶ American students are encouraged to <u>develop creativity</u> and come up with a novel method to address issues.
美國人鼓勵學生發揮創意、尋找新的方法解決問題。

例句❷ You'll see a variety of different examples, and hopefully these will help to <u>spark creativity</u> for your own design work.
你將看到各類不同的例子,希望它們能激發你設計作品的創意。

例句❸ There is limited <u>scope for creativity</u> in my job.
在工作上,我可以發揮創意的空間有限。

實用短語 / 用法 / 句型

• scope for creativity 發揮創意的空間

Crisis 危機

▶ MP3-031

Adj. + crisis

acute / grave crisis	嚴重的危機
deepening / mounting / unfolding crisis	日益嚴重的危機
impending / looming crisis	潛在的危機
financial crisis	金融危機
fiscal crisis	財務危機
refugee crisis	難民危機
mid-life crisis	中年危機

V. + crisis

be faced with a crisis	面臨危機
be hit by a crisis	受到危機衝擊
experience / go through / suffer / undergo a crisis	遭受、經歷危機
lead to / precipitate / provoke / spark (off) / trigger a crisis	引發危機
alleviate / defuse / solve a crisis	解決危機
address / manage / tackle a crisis	處理、面對危機
overcome / ride out / survive / weather a crisis	克服、度過危機
avert a crisis	免除危機

A
B
C
D
E
F
G
H
I
J
K
L
M
N
O
P
Q
R
S
T
U

aggravate / deepen / exacerbate /   加劇、惡化危機
worsen a crisis

crisis + V.

crisis arise / erupt / hit / occur / unfold   危機出現、發生

crisis deepen / worsen   危機惡化

crisis loom   危機即將發生

▶ MP3-032

例句❶ The leader emphasizes the need to prepare for impending crises.
這位領導者強調未雨綢繆的必要。

例句❷ Many employees and their families are hit by the financial crisis.
許多員工及他們的家庭都受到這次金融危機的衝擊。

例句❸ I have no doubts that Japan will weather this crisis and come back stronger than ever.
我深信日本可以度過這次的危機並變得更強大。

例句❹ The Chinese official said the U.S. missile-defense plans would exacerbate the crisis.
這位中國官員表示，美國的導彈防禦計畫將惡化危機。

例句❺ Seven years after the global financial crisis erupted in 2008, the world economy continued to stumble.
2008 年全球金融危機爆發後七年，世界的經濟仍持續動盪。

例句❻ Because of these nations' stable budgets, their governments have the ability to support their economies <u>in times of crisis</u>.

因為這些國家有穩定的財政預算，因此它們的政府在危急時刻有能力支撐經濟。

實用短語 / 用法 / 句型

- a crisis of confidence 信任危機
- a crisis of conscience 道德危機
- at / in moments of crisis 危機時刻
- at / in times of crisis 危機時刻

A
B
C
D
E
F
G
H
I
J
K
L
M
N
O
P
Q
R
S
T
U

Criticism 批評、評論

▶ MP3-033

Adj. + criticism

bitter / fierce / harsh / severe / sharp / strident / strong / trenchant / vehement criticism	猛烈的、嚴厲的批評
constructive criticism	建設性的、正面的評論
hostile criticism	惡意的批評
fair / justifiable / legitimate criticism	合理的評論
unfair / unfounded / unjustified criticism	不合理的批評
implicit / implied criticism	隱含的批評

V. + criticism

express / make / voice criticism	提出評論
direct / level criticism (+ at sb / sth)	針對、向～提出評論
attract / draw / prompt / provoke / spark criticism	引發批評
be open to / come in for / receive criticism	接受批評
deflect / escape criticism	轉移、逃避批評
silence / suppress criticism	抑制、平息批評
counter / reject criticism	反駁批評
address / reply to / respond to criticism	回應批評

criticism + V.

criticism center on (+ sth)　　　　批評集中在～

▶ MP3-034

例句❶ Hillary recently faced <u>vehement criticism</u> from her political rival, Trump.
希拉蕊近日來面臨政治對手川普的猛烈抨擊。

例句❷ The company quickly made a decision to <u>deflect the public criticism</u>.
該公司很快做了決策來轉移大眾的批評。

例句❸ The government is unlikely to <u>escape criticism</u> for its role in the affair.
在這次的事件中，政府也難逃批評。

例句❹ If we <u>level criticism at</u> the old lady, then she may gain sympathy from the public.
如果我們批評這老太太，她可能會得到民眾的同情。

例句❺ British government faced <u>a barrage of criticism</u> over the ballooning costs of the 2012 Games.
英國政府在 2012 年奧運會中爆增的預算受到了一連串的批評。

實用短語 / 用法 / 句型

• a barrage / storm of criticism 一連串的抨擊、批評

Decision 決定、判決

Adj. + decision

crucial / fateful / landmark decision	重大的決定
tough decision	艱難的決定
irreversible / irrevocable decision	無法改變的決定
arbitrary decision	武斷的決定
hasty / rash / snap decision	草率的決定
split-second decision	快速的決定
last-minute decision	最後的決定、臨時的決定
informed decision	有根據的、明智的決定
firm decision	堅定的決定
clear-cut decision	明確的決定
prudent decision	謹慎的決定
timely decision	及時的決定
unanimous decision	一致的決定
split decision	不一致的決定
collective / joint decision	共同的決定

V. + decision

arrive at / come to / reach a decision	做出決定
implement a decision	實施決策
reconsider / review a decision	重新考慮決定
defer / delay / postpone a decision	延遲決定
override / overturn / reverse a decision	推翻決定、判決

▶ MP3-036

例句❶ In the landmark decision, the CEO hoped to hear opinions from every member of the group.
在這重大決策中，執行長希望能聽到每個組員的意見。

例句❷ Plan ahead and don't make hasty decisions.
要事先計畫，不要倉促做出決定。

例句❸ We'll let you know as soon as we come to a decision.
我們決定之後會盡快通知你。

例句❹ We agreed to defer a decision on this issue until after Christmas.
我們同意將這問題延到聖誕節之後再做決定。

Detail 細節

Adj. + detail

crucial / essential detail	重要的細節
minor / minute / tiny detail	微小的細節
meticulous / painstaking detail	瑣碎的細節
further detail	更多的細節
gory / graphic / lurid detail	血淋淋的、 駭人的細節
exhaustive detail	詳盡的細節
exact / precise detail	確切、精密的細節
nitty-gritty / trivial detail	瑣碎的細節 （= 枝微末節）

V. + detail

go into / present details	詳述細節
disclose / divulge / pass on / reveal details	透露細節
lay out / set out / spell out details	闡述細節
finalize / hammer out / iron out / work out details	敲定細節

補充 iron out 也有消除、泯除的意思，如以下用法：
< iron out differences > 消除差異

discuss / negotiate details	討論細節

uncover details	發現、揭露細節
get / find out / obtain / reveal details	得到、發現細節
check / examine / study details	檢視細節
omit / neglect / overlook details	忽略細節
sweat the details	琢磨、擔心細節
spill details	說出、洩漏細節
amend / update details	修改細節
confirm details	確認細節

detail + V.

detail emerge	細節浮現
detail suggest / reveal	細節顯示

▶ MP3-038

例句❶ I can still remember the accident in gory details.
我仍然記得這場意外血淋淋的細節。

例句❷ Regardless of what information you seek, you can find it on Wikipedia, often in exhaustive detail.
不論你想要什麼資訊,幾乎都可以在維基百科上找到它詳盡的細節。

例句❸ We briefly mentioned a couple of complex methods, but then went into details about the simplest method.
我們大略提了幾個複雜的方法,然後詳細介紹當中最簡單的一個。

例句❹ I've got a plan ready for tomorrow morning if I can stay over tonight to work out the details.

我已經準備了一個計畫，打算明早就實施，前提是我今晚要先熬夜寫出細節。

例句❺ The devil is in the details. We should never overlook any details.

魔鬼藏在細節裡，我們永遠不可忽略任何細節。

例句❻ In giving a speech, you have to sweat the details.

演講的時候，你必須琢磨每一個細節。

例句❼ I'll give you a buzz later and fill you in on the details.

我等等打電話給你，再告訴你細節。

實用短語 / 用法 / 句型

- lay / set / spell sth out in detail 闡述細節

- fill sb in on details 為某人講解細節

- spare sb the details 略過而不告訴某人細節

- in detail 詳細地

- Don't sweat the details.
  不用為小事煩心。（= Don't sweat the small stuff.）

Development 發展

▶ MP3-039

Adj. + development

rapid development	快速的發展
accelerated development	加速的發展
continued / ongoing development	持續的發展
arrested development	停滯的發展
sustainable development	可持續性的發展
abnormal development	不正常的發展
cognitive development	認知發展
intellectual development	智能發展
adolescent development	青少年發展

V. + development

aid / encourage / facilitate / foster / promote / spur / stimulate development	促進發展
accelerate / speed up development	加速發展
initiate / spearhead development	開啟、推動發展
arrest / halt / hamper / hinder / impede / inhibit / restrict / thwart development	阻礙發展
oversee development	監督發展
trace development	追溯發展
underpin development	鞏固發展

development + V.

development occur / take place	發展進行
development continue	發展持續

▶ MP3-040

例句❶ We are committed to the <u>ongoing</u> professional <u>development</u> of all our employees.
我們致力於所有員工專業的持續發展。

例句❷ The organization has recently gone through a period of change and <u>rapid development</u>.
該組織最近經歷了一段轉變期並快速發展。

例句❸ In the future, new analytical methods will <u>facilitate the development</u> of medicine.
在未來，新的分析方法將促進醫學發展。

例句❹ The region's universities and land-based college will be essential to <u>underpin</u> skills <u>development</u>.
這個地區的大學將成為鞏固技術發展的關鍵。

例句❺ At the coming of the 20th century, Chinese literature entered <u>a</u> new <u>stage in development of</u> modernization.
隨著 20 世紀的到來，中國文學進入了一個新的發展階段，走上了現代化之路。

實用短語 / 用法 / 句型

• research and development （產品）研發（常縮寫成 R&D）

• a stage in the development of sth ～發展的一個階段

• ribbon development 帶狀發展（住宅）

Difficulty 困難、困境

▶ MP3-041

Adj. + difficulty

considerable / enormous difficulty	很大的困難
insuperable / insurmountable difficulty	難以克服的困境
inherent difficulty	固有的困境
potential difficulty	潛在的難題
practical / technical difficulty	操作上、技術上的困難

V. + difficulty

encounter / face / get into / run into difficulties	遇到困難
create / pose / present difficulties	造成困難
cope with / deal with / overcome / resolve / surmount difficulties	解決、克服困難
be fraught with difficulties	充滿困難（＝困難重重）
compound / exacerbate difficulties	加深困難
anticipate / foresee difficulties	預見困難

difficulty + V.

difficulty beset / confront / face / surround + sb / sth	～面臨困難、陷入困境
difficulty arise	產生難題
difficulty lie in sth	困難在於～

▶ MP3-042

例句❶ We are fully confident that we can <u>surmount</u> these <u>difficulties</u>.
我們相信我們能夠克服這些困難。
補充 「克服萬難」可說成 < move mountains >

例句❷ Although his peace policy received broad support, the cause for peace was still <u>fraught with difficulties</u>.
雖然他的和平政策獲得廣泛的支持，然而追求和平志業的路仍困難重重。

例句❸ Murray has <u>been beset by</u> financial <u>difficulties</u> since graduating from medical school.
Murray 從醫學院畢業後就一直面臨財務的困難。

Dilemma 困境、兩難

Adj. + dilemma

acute / real / thorny dilemma	嚴重的困境
age-old / central dilemma	基本的、常見的困境
ethical / moral dilemma	道德兩難

V. + dilemma

create / pose a dilemma	造成兩難
present sb with a dilemma	對某人造成兩難
confront / face a dilemma	面臨困境
grapple with / wrestle with a dilemma	面臨困境
be caught in / be faced with a dilemma	陷入困境
find oneself in a dilemma	陷入困境 （= 進退維谷）
resolve / solve a dilemma	解決困境

dilemma + V.

dilemma arise / occur	產生兩難
dilemma lie	困境在於～
dilemma confront / face + sb	某人面臨、陷入兩難

例句① The spread of armed conflict <u>presents us with a</u> real dilemma.

武裝衝突擴大使我們陷入兩難。

例句② In the process of modern urban development, we often <u>find ourselves in a dilemma</u>.

在都市發展的過程中，我們往往會陷入兩難。

例句③ The <u>dilemma</u> over human cloning <u>lies</u> at the heart of the ethical choices facing society.

人類複製的難題在於社會所面臨的道德選擇。

例句④ When you are <u>on the horns of a dilemma</u>, no matter which one you choose, something bad is bound to happen.

當你陷入兩難時，不論你選擇哪一邊，都會有壞事發生。

實用短語 / 用法 / 句型

• on the horns of a dilemma 進退兩難

Disagreement 意見不一、爭論、不同意

▶ MP3-045

Adj. + disagreement

considerable / serious / significant / strong / substantial disagreement	嚴重的分歧
public disagreement	大眾的爭論
fundamental / total disagreement	完全不同意
irreconcilable / unresolved disagreement	相當大而無法解決的分歧
minor / slight disagreement	輕微的分歧（＝小爭論）
bitter / sharp / violent disagreement	激烈的爭論
widespread disagreement	廣泛的分歧、意見普遍不一
inevitable disagreement	無法避免的分歧、爭論
ideological disagreement	意識形態的分歧

V. + disagreement

be in / have disagreement	有爭執、意見不一
handle / resolve / settle / solve disagreement	解決爭執
cause / provoke disagreement	引發爭論
avoid disagreement	避免爭論

| express / indicate / register / voice disagreement | 提出、表示不同意 |
| reflect disagreement | 反映分歧 |

disagreement + V.

disagreement arise / emerge / erupt / occur	產生分歧
disagreement exist	存在分歧
disagreement persist / remain	分歧繼續存在
disagreement escalate	分歧加深
disagreement center around / on + sb / sth	關於～的爭論

▶ MP3-046

例句❶ There is sometimes substantial disagreement between doctors and patients about health status.
醫生和患者對健康狀況的評估常有嚴重分歧。

例句❷ Try these 7 strategies to express your disagreement, without being disagreeable.
試試看用這 7 種方法來表達你的不同意，但卻又不惹人討厭。

例句❸ These countries' tactical differences reflect a fundamental disagreement between those who want to manage the world and those who want to transform it.
這些國家作戰策略的不同反映了想要掌管世界的國家和想要改變世界的國家意見分歧。

Doubt 懷疑、疑問

▶ MP3-047

Adj. + doubt

considerable / grave / serious / severe doubt	嚴重的懷疑
slight doubt	稍微的懷疑
gnawing / lingering / nagging / niggling doubt	揮之不去的懷疑、疑問
growing / increasing doubt	漸增的懷疑、疑問
reasonable doubt	合理的懷疑
fresh doubt	新生的疑慮

V. + doubt

raise / sow doubt	產生懷疑
cast / throw doubt (+on sb / sth)	使人懷疑～
entertain / feel / harbor / have doubt	抱持懷疑、存有疑問
express / voice doubt	提出、表示懷疑
clear up / dispel / eliminate / erase / overcome / remove doubt	澄清、消除懷疑
call / throw sth into doubt	使～遭受質疑
be open to doubt	受到質疑

doubt + V.

doubt appear / arise	產生懷疑
doubt exist	懷疑存在
doubt persist / remain	懷疑繼續存在
doubt surround sth	質疑圍繞在～

▶ MP3-048

例句❶ If the United States vetoed the resolution, that would remove any lingering doubt of U.S. complicity.
如果美國否決這個決議，將消除外界對美國共謀關係的質疑。

例句❷ She still felt the same niggling doubt: was he really telling the truth?
她對於他是否說實話仍抱持著懷疑的態度。

例句❸ Her record of dismissals casts doubt on her ability to hold down a job.
她被解雇的紀錄使她的工作能力備受質疑。

例句❹ The decision has thrown the proposed development into doubt.
這個決議使得提出的發展規劃遭受質疑。

例句❺ From the start, doubts surrounded her claim to be the missing heiress.
打從一開始，她聲稱自己是失蹤的繼承人這件事就備受質疑。

實用短語 / 用法 / 句型

• sow doubt in one's mind 使某人起疑心

• without / beyond (a shadow of) a doubt 毫無疑問、無庸置疑

• give sb / sth the benefit of the doubt 選擇相信（事情尚未明朗）

Dream 夢、夢想

Adj. + dream

pleasant dream	美夢
lucid / vivid dream	清晰的、意象鮮明的夢
erotic / wet dream	春夢
recurrent / recurring dream	一再發生的、反覆的夢
prophetic dream	不祥的、預言性的夢
lifelong / long-held dream	一生的、多年的夢想
crazy / distant / impossible / unattainable / utopian dream	遙不可及的夢想
pipe dream (= daydream = castle in the air)	空想、白日夢
unfulfilled / unrealized dream	無法實現的夢想
broken / shattered dream	破碎的夢想

V. + dream

dream / have a dream	做夢
awake from / wake from a dream	從夢中醒來
interpret a dream	解夢
cherish / have a dream	懷抱夢想
achieve / fulfill / live (out) / realize a dream	實現夢想

chase / follow / pursue a dream	追逐夢想
give up on a dream	放棄夢想
crush / destroy / shatter a dream	毀了、粉碎夢想
keep the dream alive	堅持夢想

dream + V.

dream come true	美夢成真、夢想成真
dream haunt / plague sb	夢縈繞著、折磨著某人
dream fade (away)	夢漸漸淡去

▶ MP3-050

例句❶ The real estate crash shattered his pleasant dream.
房地產的崩盤碎了他的美夢。

例句❷ Her plans for a movie career were nothing but a pipe dream.
她計劃進入影視圈簡直是在做白日夢。

例句❸ He left his job to pursue his dream of opening a restaurant.
他辭掉工作去追逐開餐廳的夢想。

例句❹ However, reality was so cruel that it shattered their dreams thoroughly.
然而現實卻是如此殘酷，把他們的夢想徹底擊碎。

例句❺ My boss offered me a salary beyond my wildest dreams.
我的老闆給我連做夢都想不到的高薪。

實用短語 / 用法 / 句型

- beyond one's wildest dreams 連做夢都想不到、意想不到

- as (if) in a dream 好像在夢裡一樣、恍若夢中

- the American dream 美國夢

Economy 經濟

Adj. + economy

booming / buoyant / healthy / prosperous / robust / sound / strong / thriving / vibrant economy	繁榮、穩定的經濟
improving / recovering / strengthening economy	復甦的經濟
ailing / depressed / faltering / flagging / sluggish / stagnant economy	蕭條的經濟
declining / dying / sagging / slumping / weakening economy	衰弱的、衰退的經濟
fragile / vulnerable / weak economy	脆弱的經濟（結構）
overheated economy	過熱的經濟
red-hot economy	火熱的經濟、白熱化經濟
competitive economy	競爭性經濟、具有競爭力的經濟
developing / emerging economy	新興經濟
market economy	市場經濟
black / illicit / underground economy	非法的、地下經濟

V. + economy

build economy	建立經濟
rebuild economy	重建經濟
bolster / boost / develop / jump-start / kick-start / spur / stimulate economy	促進、刺激經濟
invigorate economy	活化經濟
revitalize / revive economy	復甦經濟
cripple / damage / harm / ruin / undermine / wreck economy	傷害、削弱經濟
drive / fuel economy	帶動、推動經濟
fix / stabilize economy	修復、穩定經濟
dominate economy	主宰經濟

economy + V.

economy boom / expand	經濟繁榮、擴張
economy improve	經濟改善
economy go into recession	經濟衰退
economy collapse / contract / decline / fail / falter / shrink / slow / stagnate	經濟衰退
economy pick up / rebound / recover / turn around	經濟復甦、回升

A
B
C
D
E
F
G
H
I
J
K
L
M
N
O
P
Q
R
S
T
U

例句❶ We created the most <u>vibrant economy</u> the world has ever known.

我們建立了有史以來最繁榮的經濟。

例句❷ The government pledged that it would do its best to help the <u>ailing economy</u>.

政府承諾將盡力改善蕭條的經濟。

例句❸ Earnings from the <u>underground economy</u> are not included in most statistics on earnings.

大部分的收入統計數據是不包含地下經濟的收入。

例句❹ Wars and contagious diseases <u>crippled</u> the country's <u>economy</u>.

戰爭與傳染病削弱了這個國家的經濟。

例句❺ Today, tourism and shipping <u>dominate the economy</u> of Greece.

旅遊業和運輸業現今主宰著希臘的經濟。

例句❻ The former U.S. President George Bush believed the nation's <u>economy</u> would <u>rebound</u>.

美國前總統布希相信國家的經濟將會轉好。

例句❼ Agriculture was <u>the backbone of the economy</u> of the country.

農業曾是這個國家的經濟支柱。

實用短語 / 用法 / 句型

• the backbone / mainstay of the economy 經濟支柱

• a downturn in the economy 經濟衰退

• an upturn in the economy 經濟復甦

Effect 效果、影響

▶ MP3-053

Adj. + effect

decisive / dramatic / far-reaching / marked / profound / pronounced / significant effect	重大、深遠的影響
negligible effect	微不足道的影響
subtle effect	微妙的效果
full effect	全面的影響
beneficial / positive / salutary effect	有益的影響、效果
magical / remarkable effect	顯著的效果
potential effect	潛在的影響
disproportionate effect	不成比例的影響（嚴重的影響）
adverse / undesirable / ill / negative effect	負面的影響
crippling / damaging / debilitating / deleterious / destructive / detrimental / harmful effect	有害的影響
catastrophic / disastrous effect	災難性的影響
unintended effect	非預期的影響
opposite effect	反效果
immediate effect	立即性的效果

short-term effect	短期的影響、效果
long-term / permanent effect	長期的影響、效果
deterrent effect	嚇阻效果
inhibitory effect	抑制作用
side effect	副作用
chilling effect	寒蟬效應
domino / knock-on / ripple effect	骨牌效應、連鎖反應
greenhouse effect	溫室效應

V. + effect

bring about / exert / produce an effect	產生影響
suffer from / reel from an effect	受到～影響
enhance / magnify an effect	擴大影響
discount / lessen an effect	減輕影響
counteract / offset an effect	抵銷影響
analyze / assess / estimate / evaluate an effect	評估、分析影響
observe an effect	觀察效果
ameliorate an effect	改善效果、影響

recover from an effect　　　　　　從影響中恢復

eliminate an effect　　　　　　　消除影響

overestimate an effect　　　　　高估影響

underestimate an effect　　　　　低估影響

effect + V.

effect occur　　　　　　　　　　效果發生

effect last　　　　　　　　　　　影響持續

effect arise from / result from　　影響來自於～

effect disappear / wear off　　　效果消失、退去

effect abate　　　　　　　　　　效果減輕

補充 abate（v.）有減輕、減少的意思，常搭配
抽象名詞，如以下用法：< anger abate >
怒氣降低、< enthusiasm abate > 熱情減弱、
< interest abate > 興趣減弱

例句❶ The research goes on to show that parental involvement in reading has a more <u>marked effect</u> on a child's ability than any other factor—including social background and class.

研究顯示，比起家庭背景和社會階層，父母參與閱讀在培養孩子能力上有更顯著的影響。

例句❷ The dry weather had an <u>adverse effect</u> on the potato crops.

這乾燥的天氣對馬鈴薯產量造成了不良的影響。

例句❸ The country was still <u>reeling from the effects</u> of war.

這國家仍受戰爭影響之苦。

例句❹ It is said that milk will <u>offset the side effects</u> of some treatment.

據說牛奶會減緩療程的副作用。

例句❺ The <u>effects</u> of the drug usually <u>wear off</u> after a few hours.

這個藥的效果通常會在幾個小時後退去。

例句❻ He racked his brains for the whole day <u>to no effect</u>.

他苦思冥想了一整天仍然沒有結果。

實用短語 / 用法 / 句型

• to no effect 無效、毫無結果

Effort 努力、努力的成果

▶ MP3-055

Adj. + effort

all-out / concentrated / considerable / enormous / huge / massive / strenuous / tremendous effort	極大的努力
brave / heroic / valiant effort	勇敢的努力
painstaking effort	苦功、心血
desperate / frantic effort	死命的、瘋狂的努力
final / last / last-ditch effort	最後的努力
continuing / ongoing / sustained effort	持續的努力
feeble / half-hearted effort	少許的努力
fruitless / futile / vain effort	空忙、徒勞無功
worthwhile effort	值得的努力
grass-roots effort	基層的努力
concerted / joint effort	共同的努力
get-out-the-vote effort	為催票所做的努力

V. + effort

expend / make effort	作出努力
undertake effort	進行努力
initiate / launch effort	展開努力
redouble effort	加倍努力
waste effort	白費力氣
combine / pool effort	集結努力
lead / spearhead effort	帶頭致力於
frustrate / hinder / impede / sabotage / stall / thwart / undermine effort	阻撓努力

effort + V.

effort fail / fall flat	徒勞無功
effort pay off	努力得到回報
effort culminate in sth	努力以～告終

例句 ❶ That kind of job will require you a <u>tremendous effort</u>.
那種工作需要你付出極大的努力。

例句 ❷ The firemen's <u>frantic efforts</u> to save the victims from the crumbled houses touched all people.
消防員死命從瓦礫堆下救出受災者感動了所有人。

例句 ❸ There isn't much time left, so we should <u>redouble our effort</u>.
剩下的時間不多，我們需要加倍努力。

例句 ❹ Do not go sightseeing through areas of damage. You will only hamper the relief <u>effort</u>.
不要穿越災區去看熱鬧，你這樣只會妨礙救援行動。

例句 ❺ She felt desperate because all her <u>effort came to nothing</u> in the end.
她因最終徒勞無功而感到絕望。

實用短語 / 用法 / 句型

- effort come to nothing 徒勞無功
- spare no effort + (in) V-ing / to V 不遺餘力～
- make every effort 竭盡全力
- devote one's efforts to sth 盡心盡力

Emotion 情感、情緒

▶ MP3-057

Adj. + emotion

deep / intense / overwhelming / strong emotion	強烈的情感、情緒
genuine / heartfelt emotion	真摯的情感
conflicting / contradictory / mixed / tangled emotion	衝突的、糾結的情緒
complex emotion	複雜的情感、情緒
dark / destructive / negative emotion	負面的情緒
inner / innermost emotion	內在情感
pent-up / repressed emotion	壓抑的情感

V. + emotion

feel / experience emotion	有～情感
be choked / overcome / overwhelmed with emotion	被負面情緒所淹沒
be devoid / drained of emotion	缺乏情感、情感枯竭
communicate / convey / display / express emotion	表達情感
capture emotion	捕捉情感
release emotion	抒發情感
betray / reveal emotion	顯露情感
shake / tremble with emotion	因情緒而顫抖

bottle up / conceal / hold back / repress / suppress emotion　　壓抑、隱藏情感

control / manage emotion　　控制、管理情緒

cope with / deal with / handle emotion　　處理情緒

arouse / elicit / evoke / provoke / stir (up) / trigger emotion　　激起情感

▶ MP3-058

例句❶ The poem <u>reveals</u> the poet's <u>inner emotion</u> at that time.
這首詩流露出詩人當時的內在情感。

例句❷ Years of <u>pent-up emotion</u> came out as he sobbed.
壓抑多年的情感隨著他啜泣而流露出來。

例句❸ In most cases, expressions of <u>emotion</u> are involuntary; they are almost impossible to <u>suppress</u> or <u>conceal</u>.
大部分的情況下，情緒的表現是不由自主的。他們無法壓抑，也難以隱藏。

例句❹ Art is meant to <u>elicit emotion</u> and reaction.
藝術就是要能激起情緒和共鳴。

例句❺ Her performance in the play covered the whole <u>gamut of emotions</u>.
她在劇中的演出涵蓋了各式複雜的情緒。

實用短語 / 用法 / 句型

• emotions run high 情緒高漲、激動

• a gamut / range / roller coaster / spectrum of emotions
各式複雜的情緒

• a flood / rush / surge / wave of emotion 大量的情感

• a flicker / hint / trace of emotion 一絲的情感

Emphasis 強調、重視

Adj. + emphasis

considerable / great / heavy / huge emphasis	大量的強調
little emphasis	鮮少的強調
growing / increasing emphasis	日益增加的重視
current emphasis	當前強調的重點
particular / special / specific emphasis	特別的強調
excessive / undue emphasis	過度的強調、重視

V. + emphasis

lay / place / put emphasis (+ on)	強調、給予重視
have / receive emphasis	受到重視
change / shift emphasis	轉換重點、重視

emphasis + V.

emphasis move / shift (+ from A to B)	重點轉移
emphasis fall on sth	重點擺在某事上

例句❶ In the meeting, we discussed where the <u>current emphasis</u> should be placed.

開會時，我們討論了目前的重點應該擺在哪裡。

例句❷ I believe the education system <u>puts undue emphasis on</u> exam results and ignores learning process.

我認為教育體制過度強調考試結果，而忽略學習的過程。

例句❸ The candidate <u>shifted the emphasis</u> away from direct taxation to drum up more support from young voters.

候選人將重點從直接稅上移開，以贏得更多年輕選民的支持。

實用短語 / 用法 / 句型

• a change / shift of emphasis 重點改變、轉換

Error 錯誤

Adj. + error

blatant error	明顯的錯誤
egregious / glaring / grave / grievous / serious error	嚴重的錯誤
fatal error	致命的錯誤
minor error	輕微的錯誤
common error	常見的錯誤
inadvertent error	意外的、不小心的錯誤
fundamental / schoolboy error	最基本的錯誤
experimental error	實驗上的錯誤
human error	人為錯誤
unforced error	非受迫性失誤（運動上）

V. + error

commit / make an error	犯錯
cause / introduce an error	造成錯誤
detect / discover / identify / spot an error	發現錯誤
acknowledge / admit an error	承認錯誤
correct / eliminate / rectify an error	修正、排除錯誤
prevent errors	避免錯誤
compound an error	加深錯誤、錯上加錯

error + V.

error arise from / result from sth	錯誤起因於某事
error arise / occur	發生錯誤
error abound	充斥錯誤

▶ MP3-062

例句 ❶ He made a fatal error of borrowing more than he could pay back.

他犯了一個致命的錯誤,他借了超過他能力所能償還的錢。

例句 ❷ The plane crash was caused by human error, not mechanical failure.

這場空難是人為錯誤所致,而非機械錯誤。

例句 ❸ He had committed a grave error in letting them see the document.

他犯了一個嚴重的錯誤,就是讓他們看了那份文件。

例句 ❹ The paper accidentally printed the victim's address, and then compounded the officer's error by printing her name the next day.

這份報告不小心印了受害者的地址,而隔天這官員又錯上加錯印出她的名字。

例句 ❺ As you run through the report, you will see errors abound on every page.

當你快速看過一遍這篇報告,你就會發現每一頁都存在許多錯誤。

例句 ❻ We finally found the solution after lots of trial and error.

經過反覆的試驗,我們終於找到了解決辦法。

實用短語 / 用法 / 句型

- an error in / of judgment 錯誤的決定

- an error of fact 事實的錯誤

- a margin of error 誤差範圍、誤差幅度

- see the error of one's ways 意識到、發現錯誤

- trial and error 反覆的、不斷的嘗試

Expectation 期待、預期、期望 ▸ MP3-063

Adj. + expectation

great / high / lofty expectations	高期望
low expectations	低期望
growing / rising expectations	越來越高的期望
rational / realistic / reasonable expectations	實際的、理性的期待
false expectations	錯誤、不切實際的期待
naive expectations	天真的期待
unfulfilled / unmet expectations	未能達成的期望
wild expectations	瘋狂的、不太可能達成的期望
initial / original expectations	起初的預期
prior expectations	先前的預期
common / general / widespread expectations	普遍的預期
public expectations	大眾的預期
parental expectations	父母的期望
earnings expectations	預期薪水

V. + expectation

have / hold expectations	有～期待、期望
beat / exceed / go beyond / outperform / surpass expectations	超乎預期（好）
come up to / fit in with / fulfill / live up to / match / meet / satisfy expectations	達到期望、符合預期
dampen / dash / disappoint / fall short of expectations	期望破滅（＝不如預期）
confound / contradict / defy / shatter / violate expectations	期望落空、不符預期

補充 正如同 confound 後面可以加 expectations，confound 後面也常搭配 predictions（與預期不符）

heighten / raise expectations	提高期望
lower expectations	降低期望
build / create / set expectations	造成期待、建立期望

expectation + V.

expectations grow / rise	期望升高
expectations change	期望改變

例句❶ The older he gets, the better he is at dealing with many of his <u>unfulfilled expectations</u> in life.

隨著年齡的增長,他越來越知道如何與他未完成的人生目標共處。

例句❷ Romance novels are often accused of generating <u>false expectations</u> among readers.

浪漫小說常常會因為給讀者們不切實際的期待而被批評。

例句❸ The public's response to the music <u>outperformed</u> the band's <u>initial expectations</u>.

民眾對這音樂的反應遠超乎樂團一開始的期待。

例句❹ We paid a higher price <u>in the expectation of</u> better service. However, it <u>fell short of our expectations</u>.

我們付了較高的金額,期待能獲得較好的服務,但它卻不如預期。

例句❺ They <u>have every expectation</u> of victory in the final.

他們很期待能在總決賽拿下勝利。

例句❻ It was the right decision and was wholly <u>in line with</u> people's <u>expectations</u>.

這是一項正確的決策,它完全符合了民眾的期待。

實用短語 / 用法 / 句型

- have every expectation 很期望～

- in line with expectations 與預期相同

- in the expectation of... / that... 預期～

Experience 經驗、經歷

▶ MP3-065

Adj. + experience

considerable / extensive / vast / wide experience	豐富的經驗
limited / little experience	有限的經驗
relevant experience	相關的經驗
previous / prior experience	先前的經驗
direct / first-hand experience	直接的經驗
hands-on / practical experience	實做的經驗
collective / shared experience	共同的經驗
enjoyable / exhilarating experience	愉快的經驗
rewarding experience	有意義的經驗
indelible / memorable / unforgettable experience	難忘的經驗
harrowing / painful / terrible / traumatic experience	痛苦、不好的經驗
hair-raising / unnerving / unsettling experience	可怕的經驗
nerve-racking experience	令人傷腦筋的經驗

V. + experience

offer / provide experience	提供經驗

gain / get experience	獲得經驗
broaden experience	拓展經驗
go through / undergo experience	經歷
come through / get over experience	經歷（不好的）
recount experience	講述經驗

▶ MP3-066

例句❶ We have <u>vast experience</u> in handling contracts for both employers and employees.
在處理雇主和員工合約的方面，我們擁有豐富的經驗。

例句❷ Apprenticeships are a great way to go straight into the workplace and <u>get</u> real <u>hands-on experience</u>.
見習是一個進入職場和獲得實做經驗很好的方式。

例句❸ Finding out that your child has a disability is a very <u>painful</u> and <u>traumatic experience</u> for most parents.
對大部分家長來說，發現你的小孩有殘疾是一個非常痛苦的經驗。

例句❹ She <u>recounted</u> her <u>experiences</u> and the different methods employed compared with those in Britain.
她講述自己的經驗及不同於在英國時所採用的方法。

例句❺ It was <u>quite an experience</u> being involved in running the festival.
能夠一同舉辦這個慶祝活動是個很棒的經驗。

實用短語 / 用法 / 句型

• a wealth of experience 豐富的經驗

• quite an experience 好的經驗

Feeling 感覺、情緒、看法

Adj. + feeling

glorious feeling	極好的感覺
awful / horrible / ill / sinking feeling	不好的感覺
uncomfortable / uneasy feeling	不舒服的感覺
empty / hollow feeling	空虛的感覺
eerie / odd / strange / weird feeling	奇怪的感覺
vague feeling	隱約的感覺
general / widespread feeling	普遍的感受
intense / overwhelming / strong feeling	強烈的感受
gut feeling	直覺
inner / innermost feeling	內心的感受
ambivalent / mixed feelings	矛盾的、複雜的情緒

V. + feeling

harbor feelings	懷有感覺
express / give vent to / let out / vent / voice feelings	表達、抒發感受

bottle up / bury / hold back / mask / repress / suppress feelings　　壓抑感覺、情緒

補充 bottle up 後面也常搭配 problems（隱瞞問題）

補充 mask 後面也常搭配 intentions（隱藏目的）、
　　 purposes（隱藏目的）

capture / reflect feelings　　反映感受

hurt feelings　　傷感情

spare one's feelings　　避免某人傷心

arouse / evoke feelings　　引起情緒

reciprocate / return feelings　　對情緒、情感做出回應

feeling + V.

feeling come / creep over sb　　感覺湧上心頭

feelings run high　　情緒高漲

補充 和 p.77 emotions run high 的用法相似

feelings sweep over / wash over sb　　情緒掠過心頭

feelings well up inside sb　　情緒湧上心頭

例句❶ I have <u>mixed feelings</u> about this accident.
對於這件意外，我的心情非常複雜。

例句❷ We didn't tell Jane because we wanted to <u>spare her feelings</u>.
我們沒有告訴 Jane，因為我們不想讓她傷心。

例句❸ The debate evoked <u>strong feelings</u> on both sides.
這場辯論激起雙方強烈的情緒。

例句❹ <u>Feelings</u> on the issue are <u>running high</u> in the town.
小鎮民眾對於這個議題的情緒逐漸高漲。

例句❺ I hope there are <u>no hard feelings</u> about excluding your group.
我無法讓你們這組進去，希望你們不要見怪。

實用短語 / 用法 / 句型

• warm (and) fuzzy feeling 溫暖、窩心的感覺

• no hard feelings 不要見怪

Foothold 立足點

▶ MP3-069

Adj. + foothold

firm / solid / stable / strong foothold   穩固的立足點

V. + foothold

establish / gain / secure a foothold	取得立足點 （＝站穩腳步）
maintain a foothold	維持立足點
lose a foothold	失去立足點
provide sb with a foothold	提供某人立足點

▶ MP3-070

例句❶ Britain wanted to establish a strong foothold in the Eastern Mediterranean.
英國想在東地中海建立穩固的立足點。

例句❷ The company is trying to gain a firm foothold in the European market.
這間公司嘗試在歐洲市場取得穩固的立足點。

例句❸ The company's results show it is losing its foothold in the domestic market.
這間公司的業績顯示它逐漸失去其在國內市場中佔有的一席之地。

A
B
C
D
E
F
G
H
I
J
K
L
M
N
O
P
Q
R
S
T
U

Forefront 最前線、最重要的位置

▶ MP3-071

V. + forefront

remain in / at the forefront	保持在最前線
be positioned at the forefront	被放在最前線
thrust sb / sth + into / to the forefront	將～推到最前線
bring sb / sth to the forefront	將～帶到最前線
place sb / sth + at / in the forefront	將～放在最前線
come to / move to the forefront	站到最前線

▶ MP3-072

例句❶ We remain at the forefront of research on robotics.
我們在機器人研究方面維持著領頭羊的角色。

例句❷ Our research interests are positioned at the forefront of academic debate.
我們的研究興趣是學術辯論中首先要被考量的重點。

例句❸ It is the students' strengths that are brought to the forefront and developed.
學生的能力會被優先考量並予以適當的發展。

Friendship 友誼、友好關係

▶ MP3-073

Adj. + friendship

deep / firm friendship	深厚的友情
intimate friendship	親密的友誼 （＝知心的友誼）
enduring / lasting / lifelong / long-standing friendship	長久的友誼
genuine friendship	真正的、真誠的友誼

V. + friendship

build / forge / form / strike up a friendship	建立友誼
cultivate / foster / nurture / promote a friendship	培養、促進友誼
cement / deepen / strengthen a friendship	鞏固、加深友誼
rekindle / renew a friendship	重續友誼、重修舊好
ruin / spoil / wreck a friendship	破壞友誼

friendship + V.

friendship blossom / develop / flourish / grow	友誼發展
friendship survive	友誼持續、長存

例句❶ Team sport is a healthy way to have fun and make lifelong friendships.
團隊運動是娛樂和建立長久友誼很好的方式。

例句❷ Voluntary work can help you make new friends and cement existing friendships.
志工服務可以讓你結交新朋友也能加深現有的情誼。

例句❸ I'm sure that many friendships have blossomed from the cooperative experience.
我相信許多友情在這次合作經驗中產生。

例句❹ She offended them by turning down their offer of friendship.
她因為拒絕他們的好意而傷了他們的心。

例句❺ The president accepted this gift as a token of friendship between two companies.
董事長收下了這份禮物，作為兩間公司友好的象徵。

實用短語 / 用法 / 句型

• bonds / ties of friendship 友誼

• the hand of friendship 友誼之手

• a gesture of friendship 友好的表示

• an offer of friendship 出於友誼的好意

• a token of friendship 友誼的象徵

Gap 空隙、間隔、差距、缺口

▶ MP3-075

Adj. + gap

long gap	（時間上）長的間隔
short gap	（時間上）短的間隔
enormous / huge / significant / wide / yawning gap	很大的差距、鴻溝
narrow / tiny gap	窄小的空隙
unbridgeable gap	無法跨越的差距
widening gap	擴大的差距
generation gap	世代差距（= 代溝）
wealth gap	貧富差距

V. + gap

leave a gap	留有空隙
fill / seal a gap	填補空隙
fill the gap (+ between A and B)	填補間隔
bridge / close / narrow / reduce the gap	縮小、消除差距
widen the gap	擴大差距
identify / recognize / spot the gap	發現缺口

gap + V.

gap appear / open up   空隙、差距出現

▶ MP3-076

例句❶ There is a <u>yawning gap</u> between the rhetoric and the reality.
花言巧語與現實有很大的落差。

例句❷ Our ultimate goal is to <u>close the gap between (the) rich and (the) poor</u>.
我們最終的目的是消除貧富差距。

例句❸ If you want to make progress, you should <u>identify the gaps</u> in your skills base.
如果你想要進步，你必須找出能力上不足的地方。

實用短語 / 用法 / 句型

• take a gap year
泛指高中生畢業後，不直接升大學，而是利用一年時間選擇去打工、旅遊、實習等等，以找尋並確立興趣。此傳統在英國特別常見。

• the gap / gulf between the rich and the poor 貧富差距

Ground 地面、土地、場地、領域、理由 ▶ MP3-077

Adj. + ground

rocky / uneven ground	崎嶇的地面
fertile ground	肥沃的土地
barren ground	貧瘠的土地
common ground (= common denominator)	共同點
reasonable / strong grounds	合理的、有力的理由
sufficient grounds	足夠的理由
valid grounds	有效的理由

V. + ground

hit the ground	觸地
cover the ground	涵蓋領域
have grounds	有理由

例句❶ Congress must find <u>common ground</u> on a plan that can get support from both parties in the House.
國會必須在這方案上找到兩黨理念的共同點，來獲得眾議院雙方的支持。

例句❷ We <u>had reasonable grounds</u> to believe that he was involved with the deception.
我們有正當的理由認為他涉嫌詐欺。

例句❸ After the event of Brexit, several researchers have published articles <u>covering this ground</u>.
在英國脫歐之後，許多研究員都對這個領域發表了論文。

例句❹ The company will approve a request for early retirement <u>on the grounds of</u> ill-health.
公司將批准因為健康狀況不佳而提前退休的申請。

實用短語 / 用法 / 句型

• break new ground 開闢新領域、有新的突破

• hold / stand one's ground 堅持立場

• shift one's ground 改變立場

• on the grounds of… / that...
以～為理由（前面常常搭配動詞 reject，意思是因～的原因而拒絕）

Growth 增長、成長、發育

▶ MP3-079

Adj. + growth

considerable / enormous / exponential / significant / tremendous growth	極大的成長
impressive / phenomenal / spectacular growth	驚人的成長
explosive growth	爆炸性的增長
unprecedented growth	前所未有的成長
steady / sustained growth	穩健的增長
sluggish growth	緩慢的、停滯的成長
abnormal growth	不正常的發育

V. + growth

accelerate / boost / facilitate / fuel / spur growth	促進、加速成長
inhibit / restrict / retard / stunt / suppress growth	抑制發育、生長
see / witness growth	經歷成長

growth + V.

growth outstrip sb / sth	成長超過～

例句❶ The latter half of the twentieth century <u>saw exponential growth</u> in air travel.
二十世紀下半葉，航空旅遊產業有了極大的成長。

例句❷ The government has tried in recent years to <u>inhibit</u> traffic <u>growth</u>.
政府近幾年嘗試抑制交通量的成長。

例句❸ The UK has <u>witnessed</u> dramatic <u>growth</u> in income inequality over the past 20 years.
過去 20 年間，英國經歷了貧富差距的驚人成長。

例句❹ Consumption <u>growth</u> has far <u>outstripped</u> population growth.
消費增長已經遠遠超過人口成長。

Guideline 指導方針

Adj. + guideline

comprehensive / detailed guidelines	詳細的指引
explicit / specific guidelines	明確的指引
strict / stringent guidelines	嚴格的方針
recommended guidelines	建議的方針

V. + guideline

propose / recommend / suggest guidelines	提出指導方針
draw up / formulate / lay down / lay out / set out guidelines	擬定方針
adopt / employ guidelines	採行方針
issue / release guidelines	發布方針
adhere to / meet / stick to guidelines	遵循指引
enforce / implement guidelines	實施方針
breach / flout / violate guidelines	違反指導方針

guideline + V.

guidelines apply (+ to sb / sth)	指導方針適用於～
guidelines indicate / state	指導方針指出、指引說明

guidelines require	指導方針要求
guidelines recommend / suggest sth	指導方針建議～
guidelines stipulate	指導方針規定

▶ MP3-082

例句❶ Some organizations may have quite stringent guidelines on who can volunteer with them.
有些組織在擔任志工的資格上有嚴格規定。

例句❷ The organization should issue more definite guidelines on what owners' responsibilities are.
該組織應該發布更明確的方針說明所有人的責任。

例句❸ The minister is accused of allowing the company to breach guidelines on arms sales.
這位部長被指控放任該公司違反軍火販售的規定。

例句❹ The guidelines stipulate that a student nurse work at least 12 hours in a hospital per week.
指導方針規定實習護士每週必須在醫院工作至少12小時。

實用短語 / 用法 / 句型

• a set of guidelines 一套指導方針

Habit 習慣

▶ MP3-083

Adj. + habit

annoying / filthy / irritating / nasty habit	不好的、惱人的習慣
curious / eccentric / peculiar habit	奇怪的習慣
entrenched / deeply-ingrained habit	根深柢固的習慣

V. + habit

acquire / adopt / cultivate / develop / fall into / get into / take up a habit	養成習慣
make a habit of V-ing	養成～的習慣
break / get out of / give up / kick a habit	戒除習慣
change a habit	改變習慣

▶ MP3-084

例句❶ He had an irritating habit of interrupting others.
他有一個愛打斷別人說話的不好習慣。

例句❷ Once the attitude of making excuses for one's own mistakes becomes a deeply-ingrained habit, it is very difficult to change.
這種替自身錯誤找藉口的態度一旦變成習慣，就很難改。

例句 ❸ You can cultivate the habit of being productive and achieving your goals by constantly doing so.

你可以透過持續做某件事來培養你的習慣，並使你更有效率達成目標。

例句 ❹ To many people, it's tough to kick the habit of constantly checking email, Facebook and Twitter.

對許多人來說，戒掉一直查看電子信箱、臉書和推特的習慣非常困難。

實用短語 / 用法 / 句型

• break oneself of a habit 戒除習慣

• be in the habit of V-ing 有～的習慣

• the habit of a lifetime 一輩子的習慣

• old habits die hard 習慣難改

Health 健康、健康狀況

▶ MP3-085

Adj. + health

excellent / optimum / robust / rude health	健康狀況良好
delicate / fragile / frail / ill health	健康狀況不佳
declining / failing health	健康狀況越來越糟

V. + health

look after / maintain / protect / safeguard health	注意、維護健康
boost / enhance / improve health	促進、有益健康
recover / regain / restore health	恢復健康
nurse sb back to health	照顧某人使其恢復健康
restore / return sb to health	使某人恢復健康
compromise / jeopardize / threaten health	危害健康

health + V.

health improve	健康狀況改善
health deteriorate / fail / worsen	健康狀況惡化

health + N.

health hazard	健康危害
health insurance	健康保險

▶ MP3-086

例句❶ You appear this evening to be in rude health!
你今晚的氣色不錯！

例句❷ The burden of running the factory is too heavy for his failing health.
管理這間工廠的負擔對他日益惡化的健康來說太重了。

例句❸ The veterinarians make tremendous efforts to nurse the injured deer back to health.
獸醫們盡全力照顧那隻受傷的鹿使牠恢復健康。

例句❹ Chronic stress directly affects the immune system and, if not effectively dealt with, can seriously compromise health.
長期的壓力會直接影響人的免疫系統，如不及早治療，會危及健康。

實用短語 / 用法 / 句型

• one's state of health 健康狀況

Heart 心臟、情感、核心

▶ MP3-087

Adj. + heart

tender heart	溫柔的心
hard / stony heart	冷酷的心 （＝鐵石心腸）
heavy / sinking heart	沉重的心情
contrite heart	悔悟的心
very heart	最重要的部分

V. + heart

pierce one's heart	打動某人的心、 影響某人的心情
lift / gladden / warm one's heart	暖心、使某人感到愉悅
capture / steal / win one's heart	擄獲某人的心
pour out one's heart	傾心
tear one's heart out	傷了某人的心
lie at the heart of sth	在於～的核心
cut to / go to the heart of sth	觸及～的核心
strike at the heart of sth	打擊～的核心

heart + V.

heart leap / sing / soar / swell	心情雀躍
heart ache / bleed / sink	心痛、感到難受
heart go out to sb	同情某人

▶ MP3-088

例句❶ With slightly heavy hearts, we started trying to make compromises.
我們帶著沉重的心情試著去做出妥協。

例句❷ I wanted to pour out my heart to him and tell him all that I was feeling.
我想對他傾訴心中所有的感受。

例句❸ The committee's report went to the heart of the government's dilemma.
這個委員會的報告內容觸及政府困境的核心問題。

例句❹ Our hearts go out to the victims of the 311 Earthquake in Japan.
我們很同情日本 311 大地震的受難者。

例句❺ I devoted myself heart and soul to the arduous task.
我全心全意致力於這項艱難的任務。

例句❻ He had his heart set on spending a year or so in France.
他非常渴望能在法國待上一年左右。

實用短語 / 用法 / 句型

- an affair of the heart 戀愛、愛情故事
- a change of heart 改變主意、態度
- from the bottom of one's heart 打從心底、由衷
- get to the crux / heart of the problem 直搗問題的核心
- heart and soul 全心全意地
- have a heart of gold 心地善良
- have a heart of stone 鐵石心腸
- the hearts and minds of sb 某人的全力支持
- in good heart 興致勃勃
- put one's heart into sth 致力於～
- sick at heart 心裡特別難受
- with all one's heart / with one's whole heart 全心全意地、真心誠意地
- have one's heart set on sth 非常渴望～
- lose one's heart to sb / sth 愛上～
- to one's heart's content 盡情地
- have one's heart in the right place 出於好意的
- with half a heart 不認真地

History 歷史

Adj. + history

chequered history	曲折的歷史
fascinating history	迷人的歷史
rich history	豐富的歷史
turbulent history	動蕩的歷史
contemporary history	當代歷史
oral history	口述歷史

V. + history

be steeped in history	充滿歷史（＝歷史悠久）
go down in / pass into history	名留青史
make history	創造歷史、 做出名留青史的事情
fade into history	漸漸成為歷史
trace the history (back to)	追溯歷史
chronicle / document the history	記載歷史
recount the history	敘述歷史
distort the history	扭曲歷史
reconstruct history	重建歷史

history + V.

history go back to	歷史回溯到～
history reveal / teach / tell sth	歷史揭示、證明～
history repeat itself	歷史重演

▶ MP3-090

例句❶ The building in front of us is steeped in history.
我們眼前這棟建築的歷史非常悠久。

例句❷ He will go down in history as a wise adviser and a kind man.
他將名留青史，大家會記得他是個明智的顧問也是個好人。

例句❸ History reveals that high approval ratings are no guarantee of re-election.
歷史證明高支持率並不是連任的保證。

例句❹ Many scholars think that the event changed the course of history.
許多學者認為這個事件改變了歷史的進程。

實用短語 / 用法 / 句型

• change the course of history 改變歷史進程

• a period of history 歷史時期

• the lesson of history 歷史教訓

• the rest is history 剩下的事眾所皆知、接下來的事你們都知道了

• a page in history / a slice of history 歷史重要的一頁

Honesty 誠實

Adj. + honesty

absolute / complete / total / scrupulous honesty	完全誠實
brutal / uncompromising / unflinching honesty	殘酷的、直接的坦白
refreshing honesty	令人印象深刻的坦白

V. + honesty

admire / appreciate / value honesty	讚揚誠實
doubt / impugn / question honesty	懷疑誠實
demand / require honesty	要求誠實

▶ MP3-092

例句❶ Some may be just too sensitive to survive <u>brutal honesty</u> and so it's important to be tender and gentle.
有些人很敏感，無法承受殘酷的事實，因此委婉是非常重要的。

例句❷ I have no reason to <u>doubt</u> your <u>honesty</u>.
我沒有理由懷疑你的誠實。

例句❸ <u>In all honesty</u>, the book was not as good as I expected.
坦白說，這本書不如我的預期。

實用短語 / 用法 / 句型

- honesty and integrity 誠實正直

- in all honesty 老實說

- Honesty is the best policy. 誠實為上策。

Hope 希望、期待

Adj. + hope

deep / fervent / sincere hope	熱切的希望
distant / faint / forlorn / vague hope	渺茫的希望
false / vain hope	虛假的、不存在的希望
wild hope	奢望
lingering / remaining hope	一絲希望
high hopes	很大的期望、厚望
optimistic / sanguine hopes	樂觀的期望

V. + hope

cherish / entertain / harbor hope	抱持希望
express / voice hope	表達希望
pin / place / put hopes on sth	對～寄予希望
cling to / keep alive / live in hope	堅持、繼續抱持希望
bring / raise hope	帶來希望
not hold out (much) hope	不抱希望
abandon hope	放棄希望
crush / dash / end / kill / shatter hope	摧毀、扼殺希望
carry hopes	背負期望

hope + V.

hope lie in / rest on sth	希望在於～
hope spring (up) / surge	希望湧現
hopes crumble / die / fade	希望消逝、破滅

▶ MP3-094

例句❶ The figures kill off any lingering hopes of an early economic recovery.
這份資料扼殺了經濟早日復甦的所有希望。

例句❷ We place high hopes on the project.
我們對這個計畫寄予厚望。

例句❸ I don't hold out much hope of finding a buyer.
我對找到買家這件事不抱太大的希望。

例句❹ Our hopes were dashed when plans for a stadium were refused.
當體育場的計劃被拒絕時，我們的希望破滅了。

例句❺ The doctor's report gave us only a glimmer of hope.
醫生的報告僅給了我們一絲希望。

例句❻ The arrival of firefighters is a beacon of hope to the victims.
對受災者來說，消防員的到來是一個希望的象徵。

實用短語 / 用法 / 句型

- a flicker / gleam / glimmer / ray / spark of hope 一線希望
- keep one's hopes up 抱持希望
- not a hope in hell 毫無希望、絕不可能
- a beacon / flame / sign / symbol of hope 希望的象徵、一絲希望
- not get one's hopes up 不要抱持希望

Idea 主意、想法

Adj. + idea

bright / brilliant / clever / marvelous idea	好點子
constructive idea	有建設性的主意
ingenious / innovative / novel idea	創新的點子
wacky idea	古怪的主意
crackpot / impractical / ludicrous / outlandish / ridiculous / wild idea	不切實際的點子
half-baked / hare-brained idea	考慮不周的點子
preconceived idea	成見、偏見
definite / firm idea	明確的想法
contradictory idea	矛盾的想法
newfangled idea	新奇的想法

V. + idea

hit on / think up an idea	想到點子
put forward an idea	提出點子
push (forward) an idea	推行點子
entertain an idea	抱有想法（認真考慮）
flirt with / play with / toy with an idea	懷有想法（但未認真考慮）

mull over / sleep on an idea	考慮點子
embrace / take up an idea	接受點子
dismiss / reject an idea	拒絕點子
float / pitch an idea	提出想法來詢問別人意見

補充 float / pitch 後面也常搭配 a proposal（提出提案）

bounce an idea off	向～提出想法以得到回饋並做修正
bounce an idea around	提出想法來得到回饋並修正
generate / spark an idea	產生想法
brainstorm an idea	集思討論點子
implement / take up an idea	實現點子、履行想法
put an idea into action / practice	將想法付諸行動
articulate / communicate / convey / express / get across an idea	表達想法
relish an idea	喜歡～想法
be obsessed with an idea	著迷於～的想法

idea + V.

idea come to / occur to sb	靈光一現
idea come into / pop into one's head	靈光一現
idea flash through one's brain / mind	靈光一現
idea emerge	想法浮現

idea originate with sb / sth　　　　　想法來自於～

idea catch on / take off　　　　　　想法、點子流行起來

▶ MP3-096

例句❶ Their solution is to build more airports. It is a half-baked idea.
他們的解決方法是多蓋一些機場，但這個點子並不周詳。

例句❷ She is toying with the idea of leaving her job.
她心中有辭職的想法，但沒有認真思考過。

例句❸ We meet monthly to discuss important issues and to pitch new ideas.
我們每個月開會討論重要的議題並提出新的想法和大家討論。

例句❹ They looked for simple and effective ways to get the innovative idea across.
他們尋求簡單又有效的方法去表達這個創新的點子。

例句❺ Suddenly, an idea popped into his head and he rushed over to the manager excitedly.
他突然靈光一現想到了一個點子，然後興奮地跑向經理。

例句❻ I didn't have the foggiest idea what she meant.
我一點都不懂她的意思。

實用短語 / 用法 / 句型

- be open to ideas 願意接受任何想法

- the germ of an idea 初步的想法

- not have the faintest / foggiest / slightest idea
  一點都不知道、毫無頭緒

Identity 身分、特性

▶ MP3-097

Adj. + identity

mistaken identity	錯誤的身分、認錯人
assumed identity	偽造的、假冒的身分
collective / communal identity	集體認同

V. + identity

authenticate / confirm / verify an identity	驗證身分
disclose / divulge / leak / reveal an identity	透露、公開身分
assume / steal an identity	假冒身分
ascertain / determine / discover an identity	查明確定身分
conceal / mask an identity	隱瞞身分
construct / create / define / establish / forge an identity	發展、建立特色

▶ MP3-098

例句❶ He had registered under an <u>assumed identity</u>.
他用假冒的身分註冊。

例句❷ He was released after the police <u>verified</u> his <u>identity</u>.
警察驗明他身分後,他就被釋放了。

例句❸ The company has firmly <u>established</u> its <u>identity</u> on the British high street.
這間公司已經穩固建立了自己在英國大街上的特色。

Illness 患病（狀態）、疾病

Adj. + illness

critical / debilitating / life-threatening illness	重大的疾病
mild / minor illness	小病
acute illness	急性的疾病
chronic illness	慢性病
fatal / life-limiting / incurable / terminal illness	不治之症
degenerative / progressive illness	逐漸惡化疾病

V. + illness

experience / suffer / suffer from illness	經歷疾病、患病
catch / contract an illness	染病
bear / endure an illness	承受病痛
manage illness	控制病情
get over / fight (off) / recover from illness	戰勝疾病、康復
fake / feign illness	佯裝生病
die of illness	病死
nurse sb through illness	在某人生病期間照顧他 / 她

illness + V.

illness affect / afflict sb	疾病負面影響某人
illness beset / plague sb	疾病折磨、困擾某人
illness blight sth	疾病摧殘、破壞某事
illness hit / strike sb	某人罹病
illness arise / occur	疾病發生
illness progress	病情惡化
illness handicap / incapacitate / weaken sb	疾病使某人虛弱、無法正常生活

▶ MP3-100

例句❶ I am taking vitamin and zinc tablets to <u>get over</u> this <u>illness</u>.
我服用維他命和鋅片來對抗疾病。

例句❷ She took time off work, <u>feigning illness</u> and not answering the phone.
她裝病請假沒來上班也不接電話。

例句❸ She <u>nursed</u> her father <u>through</u> his <u>illness</u>.
她陪爸爸度過生病的日子。

例句❹ Asthma is the most common <u>chronic illness affecting</u> children worldwide.
氣喘是影響全球兒童最常見的慢性疾病。

例句❺ The pain usually gets worse as the <u>illness progresses</u>.
疼痛通常會隨著病情的惡化而加劇。

實用短語 / 用法 / 句型

• the onset of an illness 生病的一開始、前期

Illusion 錯覺、幻覺

▶ MP3-101

Adj. + illusion

false illusion	虛幻的假象
grand illusion	大的幻想
mere / pure / simple illusion	純粹幻覺

V. + illusion

create / give / produce / provide an illusion	造成錯覺
be under / entertain / foster / harbor / labor under an illusion	有幻想、錯覺
maintain / perpetuate / sustain an illusion	維持錯覺、假象
dispel / shatter an illusion	消除、打破幻想

例句① The slogan <u>provides the illusion</u> that something is being done.

這個口號造成一種錯覺，讓人認為某些事情正在進行中。

例句② I <u>harbor</u> no <u>illusions</u> about the time and effort needed to solve this problem.

我明白解決這個問題需要花費不少時間與精力。

例句③ The attack <u>dispelled</u> any <u>illusion</u> that we are safe in the world.

這個攻擊事件打破了所有的幻想，我們一直誤以為在這世界上是安全的。

例句④ It turned out that their happy marriage <u>was all an illusion</u>.

原來他們幸福的婚姻全是個假象。

實用短語 / 用法 / 句型

• be all an illusion 全是一個幻覺、假象

Imagination 想像力

▶ MP3-103

Adj. + imagination

active / fertile / rich imagination   豐富的想像力

fevered / overheated / wild imagination   天馬行空的想像力

V. + imagination

excite / feed / fire / ignite / inspire /   激發想像力
spark / stir / unlock imagination

補充 unlock 後面也常搭配 potential（開發潛力）

captivate / capture / catch / grab /   引起興趣
grip imagination

exercise imagination   運用想像力

stretch imagination   延伸想像力

defy imagination   超乎想像

leave sth to imagination   留作想像

imagination + V.

imagination conjure sth up   突然想像、聯想到～

imagination play tricks on /   異想天開
run away with sb

imagination run riot / run wild   異想天開

例句① The writer's fascinating characters are the products of a <u>fertile imagination</u>.

這位作家想像力豐富，創造出許多有魅力的角色。

例句② I learned how to tell stories in a way that <u>stretched</u> people's <u>imaginations</u>.

我學到了如何說故事能延伸聽眾的想像。

例句③ It was a decidedly hair-raising story that <u>defied</u> your <u>imagination</u>.

這是一個遠超乎你們的想像而且讓人毛骨悚然的故事。

例句④ His <u>imagination conjured up</u> a vision of the normal family life he had never had.

他突然對一個從未有過的正常家庭生活產生憧憬。

例句⑤ <u>By no stretch of the imagination</u> could our little dog be called beautiful, but he is so friendly and sweet that everyone loves him.

我們的小狗稱不上漂亮，但牠相當友善可愛，所以每個人都喜歡牠。

實用短語 / 用法 / 句型

- a figment / product of sb's imagination 想像力的產物

- by no stretch of the imagination 絕不可能

- not by any stretch of the imagination 絕不可能

Impetus 推動、促進、動力

Adj. + impetus

considerable / enormous / tremendous impetus	相當大的動力
renewed impetus	全新的動力
further impetus	進一步的動力
necessary impetus	必要的動力

V. + impetus

give / inject / lend / provide impetus	注入動力、促進
create / generate impetus	產生動力
gain / receive impetus	獲得動力

impetus + V.

impetus come from sth	動力來自於～

▶ MP3-106

例句❶ The railway gave a tremendous impetus to the prosperity of the town.
這條鐵路促進了小鎮的繁榮。

例句❷ The interest shown in our town has served to create a renewed impetus in the project.
我們鎮上的利益為這計畫帶來全新的動力。

例句❸ Much of the impetus for change came from customers' opinions.
許多改變的動力來自顧客的意見。

Importance 重要、重要性

▶ MP3-107

Adj. + importance

cardinal / fundamental / immense / overriding / paramount / tremendous importance	極為重要
primary / prime / utmost importance	首要、最重要
diminishing importance	漸減的重要性
marginal / secondary importance	次要
intrinsic importance	自身的、本質的重要性

V. + importance

assume / take on importance	承擔重要性 （= 擔負重任）
attach importance to sth	重視
place importance on sth	重視
acknowledge / appreciate / grasp / note / recognize importance	承認、認知到重要性
affirm / assert / reinforce / reiterate importance	強調重要性
discount / dismiss importance	低估重要性
diminish / downplay / play down importance	降低重要性

exaggerate / overestimate / overstate importance	誇大重要性
cast / throw doubt on importance	質疑重要性

importance + V.

importance lie in sth	重要性在於～

▶ MP3-108

例句❶ I believe motivating students to learn is of <u>paramount importance</u>.
我認為刺激學生學習極為重要。

例句❷ Air force has <u>assumed</u> a greater military <u>importance</u> in recent times.
最近空軍擔負起更大的軍事重任。

例句❸ The doctor <u>reinforced the importance</u> of being honest with children.
這位醫生強調對小孩誠實的重要。

例句❹ The town's <u>importance lies in</u> the richness and quality of its architecture.
這個小鎮的重要在於其建築形式豐富且品質優異。

實用短語 / 用法 / 句型

- in order of importance 按照重要性的順序
- a matter of (grave / great) importance 重要的事情、問題

Impression 印象

▶ MP3-109

Adj. + impression

favorable impression	好感、好的印象
distorted / misleading impression	錯誤的印象
distinct / overwhelming / profound / striking impression	深刻的印象
abiding / indelible / lasting impression	長久、不可抹滅的印象
fleeting / vague impression	短暫、模糊的印象
immediate / initial impression	第一印象

V. + impression

convey / create / leave an impression	傳達、留下印象
counter / dispel an impression	改變、破除印象

impression + V.

impression count	印象很重要

例句❶ No matter how old you are, this film will <u>leave a lasting impression</u>.

不管你幾歲，這部電影都會讓你留下深刻的印象。

例句❷ Mother's love made nothing more than a <u>vague impression</u> on him for she passed away long ago.

由於他母親很久以前就去世了，母親的愛對他僅留下模糊的印象。

例句❸ When it comes to finding a partner, first <u>impressions do count</u>.

當提到找合作夥伴時，第一印象就很重要了。

Improvement 改善、改進

▶ MP3-111

Adj. + improvement

considerable / dramatic / radical / remarkable / substantial improvement	很大的改善
marginal improvement	微小的改善
appreciable / marked / noticeable / significant / tangible improvement	顯著的改善
constant / ongoing / sustainable improvement	持續的改進
incremental / progressive improvement	逐漸的改善
much-needed improvement	必要的改善

V. + improvement

achieve / secure an improvement	做出改善
deliver / produce / yield an improvement	產生、造成改善
propose / recommend / suggest an improvement	給予建議做改善
facilitate improvement	促使改進
promise an improvement	保證做出改善

improvement + V.

improvement occur / take place	有改善

例句① These proposals will make a <u>significant improvement</u> to the current position.

這些計畫案將為現況做出顯著的改善。

例句② There was a <u>incremental improvement</u> in his work.

他的作品有逐漸的進步。

例句③ If you would like to <u>suggest improvements</u> to our website, we would be happy to hear from you.

如果您願意的話，歡迎您給予寶貴的意見，使我們的網站能更加完善。

例句④ Feedback can promote learning and <u>facilitate improvement</u>.

回饋可以促進學習和進步。

例句⑤ The economy is showing <u>signs of improvement</u>.

經濟有逐漸改善的跡象。

實用短語 / 用法 / 句型

• an area for / of improvement 需要改進的地方

• room / scope for improvement 改善的空間

• signs of improvement 改善的跡象

Incentive 刺激、動機、利因

▶ MP3-113

Adj. + incentive

attractive / generous / strong incentive　　強大的動機

added / additional / further incentive　　額外的動機

adequate / sufficient incentive　　足夠的動機

tangible incentive　　明確的動機

V. + incentive

introduce / offer / provide an incentive　　給予動機

reduce / undermine an incentive　　降低動機

eliminate / remove an incentive　　消除動機

improve / increase an incentive　　提高動機

▶ MP3-114

例句❶ The aim of this system is to give suppliers a strong incentive to reduce costs.
這個系統的目的在於給予供應商強烈的動機去降低成本。

例句❷ The vouchers provide an excellent incentive for children to visit their library.
優惠券給了小孩一個去圖書館的動機。

例句❸ High taxation rates have undermined work incentives.
高稅率降低民眾工作的動機。

實用短語 / 用法 / 句型

- have every incentive 有充分的動機

- a lack of incentive 缺乏動機

Indifference 冷漠、不感興趣 ▶ MP3-115

Adj. + indifference

absolute / complete / utter indifference	完全的冷漠
callous indifference	冷漠無情
general / public indifference	大眾的冷漠
studied indifference	刻意的冷淡
apparent / feigned indifference	表面的冷淡（未必真實）

V. + indifference

demonstrate / display / express indifference	展現冷漠
feign indifference	假裝冷淡
treat / regard + sb / sth with indifference	對～冷淡、不感興趣
be met with indifference	被冷漠以待

例句❶ It is <u>a matter of complete indifference</u> to me.
對我而言，這是一件完全無關緊要的事。

例句❷ She shows a <u>callous indifference</u> to the suffering of others.
她冷漠無情地看待他人受苦受難。

例句❸ They have <u>an air of studied indifference</u> to the problem.
他們對這個問題擺出刻意冷漠的態度。

例句❹ It's <u>a matter of indifference</u> to me whether he goes or not.
他走不走對我來說無關緊要。

實用短語 / 用法 / 句型

• an air / attitude of indifference 冷漠的態度

• a matter of indifference 無關緊要的事

• The opposite of love isn't hate; it's indifference.
愛的反面不是恨，而是冷漠。

Influence 影響、有影響力的人或事　▶ MP3-117

Adj. + influence

decisive / enormous / marked / profound / significant influence	重大的影響
subtle influence	細微的影響
disproportionate influence	不成比例的影響 （常造成不符正義的結果）
adverse / destructive / pernicious influence	負面的、有害的影響
far-reaching / pervasive influence	廣泛的影響
external influence	外在的影響
undue influence	不正當、不必要的影響

V. + influence

exercise / exert / wield influence	施加影響、 對～造成影響
expand / extend / spread influence	擴大影響力
diminish / reduce / undermine / weaken influence	削弱影響
eliminate / remove influence	消除影響
gain influence	獲得影響力
counter / counteract / resist influence	抵抗影響

| come / fall under the influence | 受～（不好的）影響 |
| be independent of influence | 不受～影響 |

influence + V.

| influence extend | 影響擴大 |
| influence decline / diminish / wane | 影響減弱 |

▶ MP3-118

例句❶ They argue that film and television can <u>exert a negative influence on</u> children.
他們認為電影和電視會對兒童造成不良的影響。
補充 對～有不好的影響也可以說成 < take a toll on sth >

例句❷ Both countries are attempting to <u>extend their influence</u> in the area.
這兩個國家正試圖擴大他們在這個地區的影響力。

例句❸ Constitutional changes were designed to <u>weaken</u> Russia's <u>influence</u> in the country.
憲法上的改變是為了減弱俄國對這個國家的影響。

例句❹ After several hundred years, Rome's <u>influence</u> around the world <u>waned</u>.
羅馬在世界上的影響力在數百年後衰弱。

例句❺ The president tried to <u>bring his influence to bear on</u> the committee's decision.
總裁試著用他的影響力去左右委員會的決定。

例句❻ He was arrested for <u>driving under the influence</u>.
他因酒駕被逮。

實用短語 / 用法 / 句型

• a sphere of influence 影響範圍

• bring sb's influence to bear on sb / sth 用某人的影響力去影響～

• under the influence of sth 在～影響之下

• drive under the influence 酒駕

Information 資訊、消息

▶ MP3-119

Adj. + information

further information	進一步的消息
accurate / credible / precise / reliable information	精確的、可靠的消息
erroneous / false / misleading information	錯誤的消息
up-to-date / up-to-the-minute information	最新消息
pertinent / relevant information	相關資料
classified / confidential / sensitive information	機密資料
detailed / in-depth information	詳細資料
comprehensive / full information	完整的資料

V. + information

possess information	擁有資料、消息
communicate / convey / pass on / provide / transmit information	傳達、提供資訊
disclose / divulge / leak information	洩露資料、消息

access / acquire / elicit / extract / obtain / receive information	獲得資訊
retrieve information	擷取資訊
appeal for / request / solicit information	徵求資訊
collect / glean information	搜集資訊
dig up information	挖掘資訊
analyze / interpret information	解析資料
cover up / suppress / withhold information	隱瞞資訊、消息
absorb / assimilate / digest information	吸收、理解資料
disseminate / distribute information	散播消息

information + V.

information pertain to / relate to sth	有關～的資訊

例句❶ More detailed information can be found on the universities' websites.
更多詳細的資訊可以在大學網頁上找到。

例句❷ We don't have full information to make a decision at the present time.
我們現在沒有完整的資訊能做決定。

例句❸ Our role is to collect and analyze information, which will be used to help make decisions.
我們的工作是收集並分析資料,以便做決定。

例句❹ We can't believe that the company is withholding information about its assets.
我們無法相信這間公司隱瞞關於資產的訊息。

例句❺ The guide is packed with information about what to do in the area.
這本指南中滿滿的都是資訊,告訴我們在這個地方能做什麼。

例句❻ This book is a mine of information on the Romans.
這本書有關於羅馬人豐富的資料。

實用短語 / 用法 / 句型

• be packed with information 滿是資料

• a mine / wealth of information 豐富的資料

• a mine of information 知識的泉源

Initiative 主動的行動、倡議、開創精神、主動權

▶ MP3-121

Adj. + initiative

bold initiative	大膽的行動
high-profile initiative	備受矚目的行動
groundbreaking / innovative / pioneering initiative	開創性的行動
joint initiative	共同的倡議
fundraising initiative	募款活動

V. + initiative

launch an initiative	發起行動
implement / spearhead / undertake an initiative	著手、開始行動
be involved in an initiative	參與行動
endorse / support an initiative	支持行動
demonstrate / display initiative	展現積極性、開創精神
seize / take the initiative	把握主動機會

initiative + V.

initiative be aimed at sth	行動目的在～
initiative be designed to V.	行動為了～
initiative seek to V.	行動試圖～
initiative founder	活動失敗

▶ MP3-122

例句❶ The new service is a joint initiative by the health service and local councils.
這項新的服務是醫療衛生部門及地方議會發起的活動。

例句❷ We are about to launch a major initiative to find out people's views.
我們正打算發起一個重要的活動來了解大眾的看法。

例句❸ Candidates should demonstrate initiative and flexibility.
競選人必須展現他們的開創精神及變通性。

例句❹ He didn't sit around waiting for someone else to take the initiative.
他沒有坐以待斃等著別人把機會奪走。

例句❺ The initiative foundered because there was no market interest in urban redevelopment.
因為市場對都市更新沒興趣，這個計畫宣告失敗。

Injury 傷害、損害

Adj. + injury

multiple injuries	多重傷害
devastating / horrific / nasty / serious / severe injury	嚴重的傷害
fatal / life-threatening injury	致命的傷害
minor / slight injury	輕微的傷害
extensive injury	大範圍的、大規模的傷害
permanent injury	永久性的傷害

V. + injury

incur / pick up / sustain an injury	受傷
be hampered / plagued by an injury	受傷痛困擾
be sidelined by injury	因傷退賽、停賽
feign injury	假裝受傷
be prone to injury	經常受傷
inflict an injury	造成傷害、損傷
overcome / shake off an injury	擺脫傷害
deal with / treat an injury	治療傷害
aggravate / exacerbate an injury	使傷害加重、惡化
assess an injury	評估傷害

injury + V.

injury occur	受傷
injury heal	傷害痊癒
injury bother / plague + sb / sth	傷害困擾～

例句❶ Researchers have determined that heading a football can cause <u>permanent injury</u>.
研究人員已經確定用頭頂球會造成永久性的傷害。

例句❷ He had <u>picked up</u> a back <u>injury</u> during training.
他在訓練時傷到背。

例句❸ Fireworks can <u>inflict</u> terrible <u>injuries</u>.
煙火可能會造成嚴重的傷害。

例句❹ Although her physical <u>injuries</u> have healed, the trauma of that day will remain with her for a long time.
雖然她身體的傷已經痊癒，但心理的創傷將殘存她心中好一段時間。

例句❺ To <u>add insult to injury</u>, the kids laughed at the boy who fell down the steps.
孩子們嘲笑那個跌下台階的男孩，這無疑是在他的傷口上灑鹽。

實用短語 / 用法 / 句型

• add insult to injury 在傷口上灑鹽、雪上加霜

Inspiration 靈感、啟發靈感的人事物

▶ MP3-125

Adj. + inspiration

fresh / original inspiration	新的、原創的靈感

V. + inspiration

derive / draw / gain inspiration	獲得靈感
look for / seek (for) inspiration	找靈感
serve as an inspiration	當作靈感

inspiration + V.

inspiration hit / strike	靈感突然出現

▶ MP3-126

例句❶ The poet <u>derived inspiration</u> from the charming scene.
詩人從這動人的景色中獲得創作的靈感。

例句❷ My best ideas and <u>inspiration</u> always <u>hit</u> me whenever I'm away from my work.
我最好的點子和靈感總是在非工作時間出現。

例句❸ There were three main <u>sources of inspiration</u> for her art: the sea, the landscape, and wild flowers.
她藝術品的靈感來源主要有三個：海洋、風景，還有野花。

A
B
C
D
E
F
G
H
I
J
K
L
M
N
O
P
Q
R
S
T
U

實用短語 / 用法 / 句型

- a flash of inspiration 靈光一現
- a spark of inspiration 靈感的火花
- a source of inspiration 靈感的來源

Integrity 正直、操守、完整性

▶ MP3-127

Adj. + integrity

absolute / high integrity 極為正直

unimpeachable / unquestionable integrity 毫無疑問的正直

territorial integrity 領土的完整

V. + integrity

doubt / question integrity 懷疑正直

maintain / retain integrity 保持操守、完整性

compromise / undermine integrity 損害正直、操守、完整性

jeopardize / threaten integrity 危及操守、完整性

▶ MP3-128

例句❶ The minister is well known to be a person of unimpea-chable integrity.
大家都知道部長是一位非常正直的人。

例句❷ The smallest mistake can undermine the integrity of an entire system.
再小的錯誤都可能破壞整個系統的完整性。

例句❸ The defect did not threaten the integrity of the building.
這個瑕疵並沒有影響建築的完整性。

Interest 興趣、趣味性、感興趣的事物、利息、利益、股份

▶ MP3-129

Adj. + interest

active / avid / consuming / deep / keen / passionate interest	強烈的興趣
slightest interest	完全不感興趣
abiding / long-standing interest	持續不變的興趣
lifelong interest	一輩子的興趣
wide-ranging interest	廣泛的興趣
intrinsic interest	內在的、本身的趣味
common / mutual interests	共同的利益
competing / conflicting / contradictory interests	相衝突的利益
vested interest	既得利益

V. + interest

evince / express an interest	表現興趣
take an interest (+ in)	對～有興趣
feign interest	假裝有興趣
arouse / drum up / generate / kindle / pique / spark / stimulate interest	引起興趣
maintain / sustain interest	維持興趣
hold no interest	不感興趣、無趣

pursue an interest	追求感興趣的事物
act in / serve interests	為～利益服務
act against interests	違背利益
represent interests	代表～的利益
defend / look after / safeguard interests	維護、捍衛利益

interest + V.

| interest flag / wane | 興趣減弱 |
| interest accrue | 利息增加、累積 |

▶ MP3-130

例句❶ With U.S. consumers watching their wallets amid economic uncertainty, the low prices may <u>pique</u> their <u>interest</u>.
如今美國經濟不景氣，人人都捏緊荷包，低價商品可能會引起消費者的興趣。

例句❷ A good leader should <u>act in the interests</u> of all his people.
一位好的領導者要為人民的利益服務。

例句❸ They were searching for the best way to <u>defend the interests</u> of the nation.
他們在找尋維護國家利益最好的方式。

例句❹ His <u>interest</u> in music has <u>waned</u> since he left university.
自從離開大學後，他對音樂的興趣就減弱了。

例句⑤ It is in your best interests to resign now.
現在辭職對你有利。

例句⑥ The event showed that the Taliban didn't have Pakistani interests at heart.
這個事件顯示塔利班並沒有將巴基斯坦人的利益放在心上。

實用短語 / 用法 / 句型

- be in sb's best interests 對某人有利
- have sb's (best) interests at heart 將某人的利益放在心上

Interview 會見、採訪、面試

▶ MP3-131

Adj. + interview

face-to-face interview	面對面訪談
extensive / in-depth interview	深度訪談
follow-up interview	後續採訪
exclusive interview	獨家專訪
press interview	新聞媒體採訪
job interview	工作面試

V. + interview

carry out / conduct / do an interview	做採訪、進行訪談
arrange / schedule an interview	安排採訪
request an interview	請求給予採訪
attend an interview	參加面試

▶ MP3-132

例句❶ In an exclusive interview with our paper, the singer admitted that he had taken drugs.
在我們報社的獨家專訪中,這位歌手坦承自己曾經吸毒。

例句❷ In the majority of cases the interviews were conducted in the respondent's home.
大部分的情況下,採訪都會在被告的家中進行。

例句❸ The newspaper requested an interview with the new president after the election.
這間報社在選後請求採訪新任總統。

Intuition 直覺

▶ MP3-133

Adj. + intuition

pure intuition	純粹直覺

V. + intuition

follow / rely on intuition	依靠直覺
confirm an intuition	證實直覺感知的事

intuition + V.

intuition guide sb	直覺指引某人
intuition tell sb	直覺告訴某人

▶ MP3-134

例句❶ Some business decisions are guided by pure intuition.
有些商業決策純粹依靠直覺。

例句❷ The results of the survey confirmed our intuitions.
調查結果證實了我們直覺認為的事。

例句❸ Jason thought his intuition was telling him that his girlfriend had been cheating on him.
Jason 直覺認為女朋友一直讓他戴綠帽。

Journey 旅行

Adj. + journey

round-trip journey	往返的旅程
arduous / exhausting / grueling journey	艱鉅、費力的旅行
harrowing journey	悲慘、痛苦的旅行
adventurous / eventful journey	驚險的、充滿變化的旅程
hazardous / perilous / treacherous journey	危險的旅程
wasted journey	白跑一趟

V. + journey

go on / undertake a journey	去旅行
embark on / set off on / set out on a journey	展開旅程
resume a journey	繼續旅程
survive a journey	撐過旅程、從旅程中存活下來
break a journey	中途短暫地暫停旅程

例句❶ She wrote a letter to her father telling him why she was <u>undertaking</u> this <u>perilous journey</u>.

她寫了一封信告訴爸爸為什麼她要去這趟危險的旅行。

例句❷ I'm sorry that you had a <u>wasted journey</u>.

我很抱歉讓你白跑了一趟。

例句❸ Drivers are advised to check road conditions before <u>setting off on journeys</u>.

駕駛人在出門前最好先查看路況。

例句❹ They <u>broke</u> their <u>journey</u> in Thailand, before flying back to Hong Kong.

飛回香港的途中,他們在泰國做短暫停留。

實用短語 / 用法 / 句型

- a leg / stage of a journey 旅行中的一段旅程
- a journey into the unknown 未知的旅程

Judgment 判決、看法、判斷　　▸ MP3-137

Adj. + judgment

accurate judgment	正確的判斷
definitive / final judgment	最終的判決
subjective judgment	主觀的判決
impartial / independent / objective judgment	公正客觀的判決
balanced judgment	考慮周全的、公正的判決
informed judgment	有根據的判斷
hasty / snap judgment	倉促的、草率的評斷
harsh judgment	苛刻的評斷
intuitive judgment	直覺的判斷
shrewd / sound judgment	精明的判斷

V. + judgment

come to / form / make / reach judgment	做出判決、評斷
deliver / pass / render judgment	表達判決、評論
reserve / suspend / withhold judgment	不做評論
exercise judgment	運用判斷力
color / cloud / distort / impair judgment	負面影響判斷

doubt / question judgment　　　　　　懷疑判斷

sit in judgment on sb　　　　　　　　評論某人

▶ MP3-138

例句① She succeeded, more by luck than sound judgment.
她成功靠的大多是運氣而不是精明的判斷。

例句② It's difficult to form a judgment when you don't have all the facts.
在沒有全部真相時，你很難做出判決。

例句③ He never allows any prejudices to cloud his judgment.
他從不讓任何的偏見影響他的判斷。

例句④ The inspector's function is not merely to pass judgment, but also to suggest improvements.
檢查員的作用不僅在於評斷，也要能提出改進的建議。

例句⑤ She felt he had no right to sit in judgment on someone he had only just met.
她認為他沒有權利去評論一個才剛剛認識的人。

例句⑥ The court delivered a judgment in the defendant's favor.
法院宣判了一個對被告有利的判決。

實用短語 / 用法 / 句型

- judgment in sb's favor 對某人有利的判決

- value judgment 價值判斷

- an error of judgment 判斷的錯誤

Knowledge 知識、了解

▶ MP3-139

Adj. + knowledge

encyclopedic / extensive / vast knowledge	廣泛的知識
in-depth knowledge	深入的知識、認識
profound knowledge	淵博的知識
comprehensive / thorough knowledge	完全的認識、了解
unrivalled knowledge	無人能敵的知識、了解
limited / superficial knowledge	有限的、粗淺的了解
rudimentary knowledge	初步的認識
up-to-date knowledge	最新的知識
inside knowledge	內部的了解

V. + knowledge

possess knowledge	擁有知識、了解
accumulate knowledge	累積知識
acquire / gain / glean knowledge	獲得知識
advance / broaden / build on / deepen / enhance / expand / extend / further / widen knowledge	增加、拓展知識
absorb / assimilate / soak up knowledge	吸收知識
brush up (on) one's knowledge (+ of a subject)	複習知識

apply / draw on knowledge	運用知識
disseminate knowledge	傳播知識
impart / pass on knowledge	傳授知識
show off knowledge	賣弄知識

補充 要記得英文裡面沒有 learn knowledge 的用法喔！

▶ MP3-140

例句❶ I have studied French for three months, but I have only a superficial knowledge of it.
我已經學法文三個月了，但我對它仍只有粗淺的了解。

例句❷ You will acquire practical knowledge and skills of all aspects of the job in the internship.
在實習期間，你會學到工作的實務知識與技能。

例句❸ I hope to further my knowledge of languages by studying Spanish at university.
我希望在大學時能學西班牙語，增加語言知識。

例句❹ The volunteers' task is to disseminate the knowledge of how to prevent the disease.
志工的任務是宣導如何防治疾病。

例句❺ There are still gaps in my knowledge of English.
我對英語的了解仍有待加強。

例句❻ They went on vacation, safe in the knowledge that the farm would be well cared for a while they were away.
他們知道出門的那段期間農場會有人幫忙管理，所以他們放心去度假。

例句❼ To the best of my knowledge, the company was originally a small workshop set up in 1978.
就我所知，這間公司起初是一家創立於 1978 年的小工廠。

實用短語 / 用法 / 句型

- a wealth of knowledge 豐富的知識
- a gap in one's knowledge 知識的落差、缺口
- safe / secure in the knowledge that~ 知道～而感到放心
- the pursuit of knowledge 追求知識
- to the best of one's knowledge 就某人所知道的
- come to one's knowledge 被某人得知、知悉

Learning 學習、學問

Adj. + learning

effective learning	有效的學習
lifelong learning	終身學習
rote learning	死記硬背的學習
higher learning	高等教育
great learning	淵博的學識
book learning	書本知識

V. + learning

facilitate / promote learning	促進學習

▶ MP3-142

例句❶ The college is dedicated to <u>promoting lifelong learning</u>.
這所大學致力於推廣終身學習。

例句❷ It is undeniable that he is a teacher with <u>great learning</u>.
我們不可否認，他是一位學問淵博的老師。

實用短語 / 用法 / 句型

• a seat of learning 學術研究的場所

Liberty 自由、自由權

▶ MP3-143

Adj. + liberty

civil liberty	公民自由
complete liberty	完全的自由
basic / fundamental liberty	基本的自由權

V. + liberty

defend / guarantee / preserve / protect / safeguard liberty	保護、保障自由
erode / undermine / violate liberty	侵犯自由
encroach / infringe + on / upon liberty	侵犯自由
curtail / restrict liberty	限制自由
endanger / threaten liberty	危及自由
secure / win liberty	獲得自由
allow sb liberty	給予某人自由
deprive sb of liberty	剝奪某人自由

例句❶ A growing climate of mistrust and fear in the country is damaging national unity and eroding civil liberties.
不信任與恐懼的氣圍上升，正破壞著民族的團結也損害公民的自由。

例句❷ The new policy infringes on our personal liberty.
新政策侵犯我們的個人自由。

例句❸ The city won its liberty in the 16th century.
這個城市在 16 世紀時獲得獨立。

例句❹ The system allows us complete liberty to do the task as we like.
這個體制讓我們有完全的自由決定如何執行任務。

實用短語 / 用法 / 句型

• an infringement of liberty 自由權的侵犯

Limit 限制

Adj. + limit

maximum / upper limit	上限
minimum limit	下限
severe / strict / stringent / tight limit	嚴格的限制
arbitrary limit	武斷的限制
agreed / prescribed / specified limit	規定的限制
recommended limit	建議的限制
acceptable limit	允許限度

V. + limit

breach / break / violate a limit	打破限制
exceed / go over / transcend a limit	超越限制
obey / observe a limit	遵守限制
define / determine / impose / place / put / set / specify a limit	限制、訂定界線
raise a limit	提高限度、額度
reduce the limit	減低限制
enforce a limit	實施限制
approach / reach the limits	接近、到達極限
explore the limits	探索極限

push / stretch / test the limits　　　　挑戰極限

push sb to the limit　　　　把某人推到極限

▶ MP3-146

例句❶ In this country, stringent limits are set on the levels of lead in drinking water.
在這個國家，飲用水的鉛含量受到嚴格限制。

例句❷ The recommended daily limit for a woman is 70g of fat.
婦女每日脂肪建議攝取量限制在 70 公克。

例句❸ In some situations, you can ask your credit card provider to temporarily raise your limit.
在某些狀況下，你可以請求信用卡公司暫時提高卡片額度。

例句❹ There are now no limits imposed on importing tobacco and alcohol products from one EU country to another.
目前在兩個歐盟國家間，菸酒製品沒有進口限制。

例句❺ The designers continue to push the limits of technology in order to create something new.
為了創新，設計師不斷挑戰科技的極限。

實用短語 / 用法 / 句型

• You are your own limit.
你是你自己的限制。（意味著所有的限制都是由自己而來，只要不為自己設限，則人有無限可能）

Market 市場、市集

▶ MP3-147

Adj. + market

competitive / crowded / tough market	競爭激烈的市場
booming / buoyant / healthy / thriving market	繁榮的、景氣好的市場
profitable market	有利可圖的市場
depressed / sluggish / weak market	景氣蕭條的市場
volatile market	不穩定的市場
black / illegal market	黑市
domestic market	國內市場
overseas market	海外市場
emerging market	新興市場
potential market	潛在市場
expanding / growing market	成長中的市場
burgeoning market	迅速成長的市場
huge / mass / sizable market	相當大的市場
niche market	利基市場
open-air / street market	露天市集
covered / indoor market	室內市集

V. + market

break into / penetrate a market	進入市場、 加入競爭市場
capture / dominate / drive / lead a market	佔領、主導市場
corner / monopolize a market	壟斷市場
bring sth to / put sth on a market	將～放到市場上
take sth off / withdraw sth from a market	將～從市場上撤掉
appear on / come on / hit / reach a market	上市、出現在市場上
flood / saturate a market	充斥市場
deregulate / liberalize a market	使市場自由化
disrupt / distort a market	造成市場混亂
capitalize on / exploit / tap into a market	利用、開發市場
stabilize a market	穩定市場
aim at / cater for / target a market	鎖定、主打市場

market + V.

market open up	市場開放
market pick up / recover	市場景氣復甦
market be up / boom / rise	市場景氣上升
market shrink	市場萎縮

market be down / decline / fall / slow	市場景氣下滑
market collapse / crash / fail / slump	市場衰退、崩解
market bottom (out)	市場衰退到谷底
market evolve / mature	市場發展、成長
market demand / dictate sth	市場需要～

▶ MP3-148

例句❶ In a highly <u>competitive market</u>, pharmaceutical companies are under intense pressure to increase efficiency.

在高度競爭的市場中，製藥公司有極大的壓力必須提升製藥效率。

例句❷ A relatively small group of collectors <u>drives</u> the art <u>market</u>.

一小群收藏家主導著藝品市場。

例句❸ The company is attempting to <u>tap into a</u> new <u>market</u> for their products.

這間公司正嘗試開發新的市場來增加產品銷售量。

例句❹ What happens next will depend very much on whether the <u>market picks up</u> in August.

下一步的發展將端看八月份的市場景氣是否能復甦。

例句❺ The <u>market</u> is continuously <u>evolving</u> to ensure magazines carry on appealing to their target audience.

市場不斷做調整，以確保雜誌能繼續迎合目標客群的需求。

例句❻ Most people <u>are not in the market for</u> this kind of product.

大部分的人對這項產品不感興趣。

例句❼ Rising mortgage rates will <u>price</u> some people <u>out of the market</u>.

抵押貸款利息上升會使人們沒有意願借貸。

實用短語 / 用法 / 句型

- the bottom drops / falls out of the market 市場崩解
- be in the market for sth 有興趣購買～
- a gap in the market 市場的空缺（= 商機）
- price sb out of the market （價格太高）使人沒有意願購買
- a drug on the market 滯銷商品、供應過剩的商品
- bear market 熊市（呈現下滑趨勢的金融市場）
- bull market 牛市（呈現上漲趨勢的金融市場）

Marriage 婚姻、婚禮

Adj. + marriage

disastrous / stormy / tempestuous / troubled marriage	糟糕的婚姻
broken / failed marriage	失敗、破裂的婚姻
stable / strong marriage	穩固的婚姻
sham marriage	假結婚
homosexual / same-sex marriage	同性婚姻
common-law marriage	同居婚姻 （未經法律登記的婚姻）
arranged marriage	被安排的婚姻、 相親而成的婚姻
forced marriage	被強迫的婚姻、逼婚
civil marriage	公證結婚
shotgun marriage	奉子成婚的婚禮

V. + marriage

enter into a marriage	步入婚姻
annul / dissolve / terminate a marriage	結束婚姻
destroy / doom / ruin / wreck a marriage	摧毀婚姻
contemplate / intend marriage	打算結婚
propose marriage (+ to sb)	求婚

recognize marriage	承認婚姻
consummate / solemnize a marriage	完婚
ban / forbid / prohibit a marriage	禁止婚姻

marriage + V.

marriage break down / break up / collapse / crumble / disintegrate / fall apart / founder	婚姻破裂
marriage take place	舉行婚禮

▶ MP3-150

例句① With more financial independence, women would not have to be trapped in a violent and abusive <u>marriage</u>.
經濟獨立後，女人就不會被困在暴力與惡言相向的婚姻當中。

例句② We wish them well for the future and hope they enjoy a <u>stable marriage</u>.
我們祝他們未來一切安好，也希望他們有一個穩定的婚姻。

例句③ His obsessive behavior <u>wrecked</u> his <u>marriage</u>.
他過於執著的行為毀了他的婚姻。

例句④ He criticized the government's refusal to <u>recognize same-sex marriages</u>.
他批評政府拒絕承認同性婚姻。

例句⑤ When the boy was three, his parents' <u>marriage broke down</u> and his father left.
這男孩三歲的時候父母離異，爸爸就離開家了。

實用短語 / 用法 / 句型

• ask for sb's hand in marriage 向～求婚

• win sb's hand in marriage 成功向～求婚

• a marriage of convenience 基於利害關係的婚姻

Media 媒體

Adj. + media

mass media	大眾媒體
mainstream media	主流媒體
print media	印刷、平面媒體
digital media	數位媒體
news media	新聞媒體

V. + media

control / manipulate the media	操縱媒體
dominate the media	主宰媒體、 在媒體中佔重要地位
exploit / handle the media	利用媒體

media + V.

media cover / report sth	媒體報導
media pick up on sth	媒體注意到某事
media portray sb / sth	媒體描述

例句❶ The story has <u>dominated the media</u> for almost a week.
這則報導已經佔據媒體版面將近一個禮拜。

例句❷ <u>Handled</u> well, the <u>media</u> is a useful vehicle for getting your message across.
如果被妥當運用的話,媒體是一個能有效傳播訊息的媒介。

例句❸ I think the <u>media picked up on</u> the story because the victim was a woman.
我認為媒體會注意到這則報導是因為受害者是一名婦人。

實用短語 / 用法 / 句型

- access to the media 使用媒體的機會、權利
- media baron / mogul / tycoon 媒體大亨
- media coverage 媒體報導
- media attention / spotlight 媒體焦點
- media darling 媒體寵兒

Meeting 會議、會面

Adj. + meeting

forthcoming / upcoming meeting	即將到來的會議
clandestine / confidential / close-door / secret meeting	私下的、機密的會議
preliminary / preparatory meeting	預備、籌備會議
protracted meeting	漫長的會議
general meeting	全體大會
interim meeting	臨時會議
virtual meeting	虛擬會議 （= 視訊會議）
chance / unexpected meeting	邂逅、巧遇

V. + meeting

attend a meeting	出席會議
call for / demand a meeting	要求開會
arrange / call / convene / hold / schedule a meeting	安排、召集會議
summon sb to a meeting	召集某人開會
chair / conduct / host / preside over a meeting	主持會議

run a meeting	進行會議
call a meeting to order	宣布開始開會
call off / cancel a meeting	取消會議
defer / postpone a meeting	延後會議
adjourn a meeting	休會
conclude / dismiss a meeting	結束會議
bring / draw a meeting to an end	終止會議
address / report to a meeting	在大會上作演說、報告

meeting + V.

meeting take place	會議舉行
meeting commence / open	會議開始
meeting break up / conclude	會議結束

例句① The preliminary meeting of the sporting event will be held on the 20th of January.

運動賽事的籌備會將在一月二十號舉行。

例句② The committee will call a meeting to discuss the president's death.

委員會將召開會議討論總裁過世一事。

例句③ It is still unclear whether the meeting will take place as planned.

目前仍不清楚會議是否會照常舉行。

例句④ The meeting officially broke up at around ten o'clock.

會議在十點左右正式結束。

例句⑤ Even after a protracted meeting, they still failed to reach a meeting of the minds.

即使在漫長的會議後，他們仍無法達成共識。

實用短語 / 用法 / 句型

- the minutes of a meeting 會議記錄
  (= meeting minutes)
- a meeting of (the) minds 理解彼此、意見一致

Memory 回憶、記憶力

▶ MP3-155

Adj. + memory

fond / lovely / sweet memory	很棒的回憶
bitter / painful / traumatic memory	痛苦的回憶
poignant memory	辛酸的回憶
dim / distant / faint / foggy / hazy / vague memory	模糊的回憶
abiding memory	難忘的回憶
haunting memory	揮之不去的回憶
repressed memory	被壓抑的回憶
excellent / retentive memory	很好的記憶力

V. + memory

bring back / conjure up / evoke / invoke / stir / trigger a memory	喚起回憶
block out / bury / erase / repress / suppress a memory	忘卻、壓抑回憶
recount a memory	講述回憶
enhance / improve / strengthen memory	增強記憶力
refresh one's memory	使某人恢復記憶
be etched in memory	刻印在記憶中

escape one's memory	逃脫某人的記憶 （＝記不得～）
commit sth to memory	記住某事

memory + V.

memory linger / live on	回憶徘徊、繼續存在
memory come flooding back / flood back	回憶湧現
memory fail sb	某人忘記～

▶ MP3-156

例句❶ The photo brought back his memories of the years at California with his family.
這張照片勾起他那些年和家人在加州生活的回憶。

例句❷ She decided to move house to erase her painful memories of her ex-boyfriend.
為了忘記和前男友痛苦的回憶，她決定搬家。

例句❸ I committed the number to memory and threw the letter away.
我記住數字後就把信丟了。

例句❹ When we visited my old family home, memories came flooding back.
當我們回到老家，以前的回憶都湧上心頭。

例句❺ The team won the title in 1997, if my memory serves me right.

我記得沒錯的話，這支隊伍在 1997 年贏得冠軍。

例句❻ The spectacular scene is burned into my memory.

那壯麗的景色深深烙印在我腦中。

實用短語 / 用法 / 句型

• memory plays tricks (on sb) 記憶開某人玩笑（＝某人記錯）

• if my memory serves me (well / right / correctly) 如果我記得沒錯的話

• in / within living memory 在現今人們的記憶中

• sth be burned into one's memory 對～印象深刻、某事深深烙印在腦中

Message 消息、訊息、寓意、要旨　▶ MP3-157

Adj. + message

cryptic message	難理解的訊息
urgent message	緊急訊息
stark / unambiguous message	鮮明清楚的消息、寓意
conflicting / confusing / contradictory message	相互矛盾、衝突的寓意
core message	主旨
hidden / subliminal message	隱含的訊息、言外之意

V. + message

leave a message	留下訊息
take a message	幫某人留訊息、轉達訊息
carry / convey / transmit a message	傳遞訊息
bring home / ram home / reinforce a message	強調主旨、訊息
disseminate / preach / spread a message	傳播、宣傳訊息

message + V.

message pop up　　　　　　　　　　訊息彈出

message reach sb　　　　　　　　　訊息傳達到某人

▶ MP3-158

例句❶ The government sent out a <u>stark message</u> about the importance of school attendance.
政府清楚傳達就學的重要。

例句❷ We <u>are</u> constantly bombarded with <u>conflicting</u> <u>messages</u> regarding image and diet.
我們不斷受形象與飲食這兩個相衝突的訊息所困擾。

例句❸ The campaign aims to <u>bring home the message</u> that drinking and driving is dangerous.
這個活動的主旨是強調酒後開車很危險。

例句❹ Unfortunately, the <u>message</u> didn't <u>reach</u> me in time.
我不幸沒能及時收到這個消息。

實用短語 / 用法 / 句型

• answer phone / voice message 語音留言訊息

Mind 頭腦、智力、意見

Adj. + mind

creative / fertile / imaginative mind	想像力豐富的頭腦
active mind	靈活的頭腦
keen / quick / sharp mind	敏銳的頭腦
curious / enquiring / inquisitive mind	好問的精神
logical / rational mind	邏輯、理性思維
dirty / perverted / sick / twisted / warped mind	骯髒、齷齪的想法
one-track mind	狹隘的想法、滿腦子只想著一件事
closed mind	封閉的心態
open mind	開放的心胸
suspicious mind	懷疑的態度
tortured / troubled mind	苦惱的心
deranged mind	精神錯亂
wandering mind	徘徊不定的思緒（= 心不在焉）

V. + mind

come into / come to / cross / flash into / go through / spring to one's mind	浮現在腦中、想到
fill / invade / occupy one's mind	佔據腦海、心思
concentrate / direct / fix / focus one's mind	專心
engage one's mind	投入心思
escape / slip one's mind	忘記
broaden / stretch one's mind	開拓心胸
exercise / train one's mind	訓練頭腦、思維
clear one's mind	理清思緒
empty one's mind	清空思緒、放空腦袋
free one's mind	讓思緒不受限制
boggle one's mind	使某人感到驚訝、困惑
blow one's mind	使某人感到驚訝、驚奇
haunt / plague / prey on one's mind	困擾某人
cloud one's mind	擾亂思緒
dull one's mind	鈍化頭腦、思維
corrupt / poison one's mind	腐化、殘害思想
ease one's mind	使某人安心
refresh one's mind	使某人清醒、提起精神
relax one's mind	放鬆心情

| lose one's mind | 失去理智 |
| read one's mind | 讀心 |

mind + V.

mind drift / wander	心不在焉
mind race	腦袋不停地思考
mind boggle / reel	感到驚訝、困惑
mind turn to sth	心思轉向～

▶ MP3-160

例句❶ To be a good journalist, you need an <u>enquiring mind</u>.
想成為一位好記者，你需要有一顆好問的心。

例句❷ When it comes to men, this girl has a <u>one-track mind</u>.
She wants to marry a rich man.
每當提到男人，這個女孩滿腦子只想著要嫁給有錢人。

例句❸ I'm sorry that I forgot your birthday—it completely <u>slipped my mind</u>.
我很抱歉完全忘了你的生日。

例句❹ Travel helps to improve your confidence and <u>broaden your mind</u>.
旅行能增加你的自信，也可以開拓心胸。

例句❺ It has been <u>preying on my mind</u> ever since it happened.
自從那件事發生後，它就一直困擾著我。

例句❻ It was difficult to <u>keep my mind on</u> my work with all that was going on around me.
周遭發生的事情讓我無法專心在工作上。

例句 7 His case was constantly <u>at the forefront of my mind</u>.
我不斷思考著他的事情。

例句 8 I still can't <u>get my mind around</u> the cruel things she said last night.
她昨晚告訴我一些殘酷的事情，我到現在仍無法理解。

實用短語 / 用法 / 句型

- keep one's mind on sth 專心於某事
- take one's mind off sth 轉移注意力
- have half a mind to do sth 有點想做某事
- bear / keep in mind 記住
- be imprinted on / stick in one's mind 銘記、烙印在腦中
- mind-boggling 令人極為驚訝的
- at / in the back of one's mind 在腦海裡但沒有付諸行動
- at / in the forefront of one's mind 不斷思考著（某事）
- a frame / state of mind 情緒狀態
- get / wrap one's mind around sth 理解某事
- have sth in mind 想到、考慮到
- in the recesses of one's mind 在內心深處
- in one's right mind 精神正常、頭腦清楚的
- mind and body 身心
- no doubt in one's mind 毫不懷疑
- put / set one's mind to sth 下定決心去做～
- make up one's mind (+ to V.) 下定決心
- uppermost in one's mind 心中最重要的
- mind is in a turmoil 思緒一團混亂

Moment 片刻、時機、重要時刻

Adj. + moment

critical / crucial / decisive / defining / pivotal / watershed moment	關鍵時刻、決定性的時刻
opportune / right moment	恰當的時機
brief / fleeting / passing moment	短暫的時間、瞬間
poignant moment	心酸的、慘痛的時刻
heart-stopping moment	驚心動魄的時刻
historic moment	歷史性的一刻
climactic moment	最高潮的時刻
unguarded moment	疏忽、不注意的時刻
senior moment	健忘（僅適合用於自嘲）

V. + moment

cherish / treasure a moment	珍惜時刻
relish / revel in / savor a moment	沉浸、享受時刻
capture / seize a moment	捕捉時刻、把握時機
recall / reflect on / relive a moment	回想時刻
hang on / hold on a moment	等一下、暫停一下
spare sb a moment	騰出時間給某人

moment + V.

moment arrive / come / occur	時刻到來、發生
moment pass	時刻、時機過了

▶ MP3-162

例句❶ The offer came at an <u>opportune moment</u> in my career.
這個工作機會來的正是時候。

例句❷ I had a <u>senior moment</u>. I cannot remember where my car key is.
我真健忘,我想不起來車鑰匙放去哪了。

例句❸ <u>In the heat of the moment</u> she forgot what she wanted to say.
一時激動之下,她都忘了自己剛剛要説什麼。

例句❹ He seemed to spend <u>every waking moment</u> of the weekend doing homework.
他似乎整個週末都在做作業。

例句❺ Jennifer's mom called her <u>a moment ago</u>, asking her to go home.
Jennifer 的媽媽剛才打給她,要她回家。

例句❻ There's <u>never a dull moment</u> in this job.
這份工作絕不無聊。

實用短語 / 用法 / 句型

- at the moment / at this point 在這一刻
- on the spur of the moment 一時衝動、立刻
- in the heat of the moment 盛怒之下、一時激動之下
- in a rash moment 匆忙之下
- at a given moment 特定時刻
- every waking moment 醒著的每一刻
- a moment ago 剛才、片刻之前
- a moment or two 一會兒
- never a dull moment 沒有無聊的時刻、絕無冷場
- not a moment too soon 來的正是時候
- the present moment 當下
- a moment of triumph 勝利的時刻

Momentum 動力、氣勢

▶ MP3-163

Adj. + momentum

considerable / great momentum	強大的動力、氣勢
irresistible / irreversible / unstoppable momentum	擋不住的動力、氣勢
fresh momentum	新的動力

V. + momentum

build (up) / create / generate momentum	製造動力、建立氣勢
acquire / develop / gain / gather momentum	獲得、累積動力
keep up / maintain / sustain momentum	保持動力
build on / capitalize on momentum	依靠、利用動力
lose momentum	失去動力、氣勢

momentum + V.

momentum build (up) / gather	氣勢建立、累積
momentum go	氣勢衰退

例句 ❶ Over the past few years, this concept has <u>developed</u> <u>irresistible momentum</u>.

過去幾年來，這股思潮已經發展出銳不可擋的氣勢。

例句 ❷ The government cannot afford to <u>lose momentum</u> at this stage.

政府在這個階段不能失去聲勢。

實用短語 / 用法 / 句型

• keep the momentum going 保持動力、氣勢

Money 金錢

▶ MP3-165

Adj. + money

spare money	多餘的錢
dirty money	非法的錢財
easy money	得來容易的錢、 不義之財
hard-earned money	辛苦賺來的錢、血汗錢
pin / pocket money	零用錢
counterfeit / fake money	偽鈔

V. + money

fritter away / squander / throw away money (+ on sth)	浪費錢
bring in money	賺錢
collect / raise money	募款、募集資金
bank / deposit money	存錢
withdraw money	領錢
divert / transfer money	轉帳
pay out / shell out money	付一大筆錢
refund money	退款

repay money	還錢
pour / pump / sink money	注入資金
put up money	提供資金、出資
pool money	合資
hoard / stash away money	貯藏、私藏錢財
tie up money	套牢、綁死資金
embezzle money	盜用資金
extort money	敲詐、勒索錢財

money + V.

money go on sth	金錢花在～上
money come in / flow in / pour in / roll in	金錢湧入

▶ MP3-166

例句❶ We shelled out an obscene amount of money for those concert tickets.
我們花了一大筆錢買演唱會門票。

例句❷ He managed to persuade his friend to put up the money for the venture.
他設法說服朋友出資創立這間公司。

例句❸ All their money was tied up in long-term investments.
他們所有的錢都被綁死在長期投資了。

例句❹ The boat trip lasts three hours, so you certainly get your money's worth.
這趟航程長達三個小時,肯定讓你值回票價。

例句⑤ They tend to <u>throw money at</u> problems without trying to work out the best solution.
他們傾向於砸錢解決問題，而不會試著去想出最好的解決方法。

例句⑥ He was charged with <u>money laundering</u>.
他被指控洗錢。

實用短語 / 用法 / 句型

- be in the money 很富裕

- bet money on sth 將錢押注在～上

- get one's money's worth 錢花得值得

- right on the money 精準無誤

- throw money at sth 砸錢解決問題

- throw one's money around 撒錢、將錢花在不必要的事物上

- have money to burn 有多到花不完的錢

- money laundering 洗錢

- hush money 封口費

- bribe money 賄賂金

- seed money 種子基金、創業基金

Mystery 難以理解的事物、神祕　　▶ MP3-167

Adj. + mystery

enduring / eternal / long-standing mystery	長久以來的謎
insoluble / unfathomable / unsolved mystery	未解之謎
deep / profound mystery	奧祕
complete / total mystery	完全、十分神祕
intriguing mystery	有趣的謎團

V. + mystery

clear up / crack / piece together / reveal / uncover / unlock / unravel a mystery	解開謎團
explore / penetrate / understand a mystery	了解、探究神祕
contemplate / ponder a mystery	思考神祕
shed light on / throw light on a mystery	解釋謎團
pose a mystery	造成神祕、謎
be cloaked in / be shrouded in / be wrapped in a mystery	籠罩在謎團之中
remain a mystery	依然成謎

mystery + V.

mystery surround sth　　　　　　　神祕圍繞著某事

mystery remain　　　　　　　　　　神祕繼續存在

▶ MP3-168

例句❶ The issue of consciousness is considered by many to be the most important <u>unsolved mystery</u> of modern science.
意識問題被許多人認為是當代科學中最重要的未解之謎。

例句❷ The novel is about the attempts of a young journalist to <u>unravel the mystery</u> of a young girl's murder 25 years ago.
這本小說講述一位年輕記者嘗試解開謎團，一宗 25 年前發生的女孩謀殺案。

例句❸ The whole incident <u>was shrouded in mystery</u>. No one knew the cause of the man's death.
整起事件籠罩在謎團當中，沒人知道男子的死因。

實用短語 / 用法 / 句型

• an air / aura of mystery 神祕的氣氛

• take the mystery out of sth 解開～的神祕面紗

• sth of a mystery 神祕的～

Myth 沒有事實根據的觀點、神話、迷思　▶ MP3-169

Adj. + myth

common / popular / prevailing / widespread myth	普遍的迷思
enduring / persistent myth	長久以來的迷思

V. + myth

debunk / dispel / disprove / explode / expose / scotch / shatter myth	破除迷思
peddle / perpetuate / propagate a myth	散播迷思
buy into a myth	相信迷思
challenge / question a myth	質疑迷思

補充 debunk / dispel / disprove / explode / expose / scotch / shatter 這些動詞後面也常搭配 rumor，< to scotch the rumor of his bankruptcy> 打破他破產的謠言。

myth + V.

myth persist / remain	迷思持續存在

例句❶ One of the most <u>enduring myths</u> about Manchester is that it always rains there.

曼徹斯特經常下雨是大家對它一個長久以來的迷思。

例句❷ Women's magazines often <u>perpetuate the myth</u> that thin is beautiful.

女性雜誌經常散播著瘦即是美的迷思。

例句❸ <u>The myth persists</u> that women are more detail-oriented than men.

女人比男人更注重細節的迷思仍然存在。

Negotiation 談判、協商

▶ MP3-171

Adj. + negotiation

lengthy / prolonged / protracted negotiations	長時間的協商
ongoing negotiations	進行中的談判
forthcoming negotiations	即將到來的協商
preliminary negotiation	初步的協商
intense negotiations	激烈的談判
tough negotiations	棘手的談判
fruitless negotiations	沒有結果的談判
face-to-face negotiations	面對面的協商
behind-the-scenes negotiations	幕後協商
bilateral negotiations	雙邊談判
multilateral negotiations	多邊談判

V. + negotiation

commence / enter (into) / initiate / open negotiations	開始協商
conduct / hold / pursue / undertake negotiations	進行協商
conclude negotiations	結束協商

break off / terminate negotiations	中止協商
reopen / resume negotiations	重新開始、繼續協商

negotiation + V.

negotiations go on / proceed	協商繼續進行
negotiations take place	談判發生
negotiations break down / collapse / fail	協商破裂

▶ MP3-172

例句① A deal was signed yesterday after weeks of protracted negotiations.
經過數週曠日廢時的談判，在昨天簽約了。

例句② We have conducted negotiations with the manufacturers on behalf of the client.
我們已經代表顧客和製造商進行協商。

例句③ The three senior executives got up and strode angrily out of the room, breaking off negotiations.
三位高層主管怒氣沖沖起身走出房間，談判也因此中止。

例句④ The union said that everything is open to negotiation.
工會表明每件事情都有協商的空間。

實用短語 / 用法 / 句型

• be open / subject to negotiation 願意協商、有協商的空間

• a basis for negotiation 談判基礎

• a matter for negotiation 有待商榷的問題

• room for negotiation 協商的空間

Niche 合適的職務、利基

▶ MP3-173

Adj. + niche

particular / special / specific / unique niche	特定的利基
lucrative / profitable niche	有利可圖的利基

V. + niche

carve (out) / find a niche	找到合適的職務
discover / find / identify / recognize / spot a niche	找到利基
carve (out) / develop / establish a niche	開拓利基
fill / occupy a niche	擁有利基
exploit a niche	利用利基
fit / serve a niche	迎合利基市場
target a niche	針對利基市場

例句❶ So far he hasn't <u>found a niche</u> where he feels he belonged.

他目前還沒找到一份適合的工作。

例句❷ Firms may respond to this pressure by specializing and deliberately <u>occupying</u> different <u>niches</u>.

公司可能會透過專業化和佔有不同利基來應對這個市場壓力。

例句❸ The company was keen to develop more products to <u>serve</u> this <u>lucrative niche</u>.

公司熱切研發更多的產品來迎合這個有利可圖的利基市場。

實用短語 / 用法 / 句型

• a niche in the market 市場上的利基、商機

Opinion 意見、看法、輿論

Adj. + opinion

favorable / high / positive opinion	好評、正面的評價
low / negative / poor opinion	負評
strong opinion	堅定的看法
conflicting / mixed opinion	對立的、不同的意見
considered opinion	深思熟慮的意見
informed opinion	有根據的意見
second opinion	其他人的意見
prevailing opinion	普遍的看法
general / popular / public opinion	大眾輿論

V. + opinion

develop / form / formulate an opinion	形成、產生看法
air / express / offer / state / voice an opinion	發表意見
venture an opinion	冒風險發表意見
canvass / seek / solicit opinions	徵求意見
get / obtain an opinion	得到意見、看法
revise an opinion	改變看法
share an opinion	同意看法

respect / value an opinion	尊重意見
influence / shape / sway an opinion	影響看法
confirm / support an opinion	證實觀點、支持看法
mold opinion	形成、影響輿論

opinion + V.

opinion prevail	看法存在
opinion differ / diverge / vary	意見分歧
opinion shift	看法改變、輿論轉變

▶ MP3-176

例句① Most students have a <u>high opinion</u> of that teacher.
大部分的學生都給予那位老師正面評價。

例句② There are <u>conflicting opinions</u> regarding genetically modified food.
民眾對基改食物有不同的看法。

例句③ The review team <u>sought opinions</u> from a wide range of those who were affected by the decision.
評估團隊徵求那些受到決策影響民眾的意見。

例句④ The defendant tried to <u>sway the opinion</u> of the jury.
被告試圖影響陪審團的意見。

例句⑤ <u>Opinions</u> on the procedure <u>diverge</u> widely among doctors.
醫生對這個醫療程序的看法分歧。

例句⑥ He has always <u>been of the opinion that</u> university students ought to have a wider range of knowledge.
他總認為大學生應該要有更廣的知識。

實用短語 / 用法 / 句型

- a difference of opinion 意見的不同

- a clash of opinions 意見衝突

- in someone's opinion 在～看來、依據某人的看法

- be of the opinion that 認為、主張

- an opinion regarding / concerning sth 關於～的看法

- opinion be in favor of sth 支持～的説法

- in one's humble opinion 以某人的淺見來看

- a matter of opinion 看法不同的問題

- climate of opinion 輿論氛圍、輿論潮流

- shades of opinion 不同的意見

- opinion poll 民意調查

- opinions are divided over sth 對某事的意見分歧

Opportunity 機會

▶ MP3-177

Adj. + opportunity

golden / huge opportunity	大好機會
rare / unparalleled / unrivalled opportunity	特別的、難得的機會
once-in-a-lifetime opportunity	一生一次的機會
unprecedented opportunity	前所未有的機會
heaven-sent opportunity	天賜良機
fleeting opportunity	短暫的機會
ample opportunity	許多的機會
future / possible / potential opportunity	可能的機會
missed / wasted opportunity	錯失的機會
equal opportunities	平等的機會

V. + opportunity

afford / allow / bring / offer sb an opportunity	給某人機會
deny sb an opportunity	不給某人機會
embrace / exploit / grasp / jump at / leap at / seize / take an opportunity	利用、把握機會
miss / pass up / squander / waste an opportunity	錯過、浪費機會
identify / spot an opportunity	發現機會
pursue / seek an opportunity	找尋機會

opportunity + V.

opportunity arise / come / knock / occur	機會出現、到來
opportunity present itself	機會出現

例句❶ This is a <u>golden opportunity</u> for us to show what we can do.
這是我們展現能力的大好機會。

例句❷ Don't <u>miss</u> this <u>rare opportunity</u> to see the best musical in the world.
不要錯過這個難得的機會去看世界上最棒的音樂劇。

例句❸ At that time, Chinese people <u>were denied the opportunity</u> to buy homes outside the Chinatown.
中國人當時被禁止在唐人街以外的地方買房。

例句❹ You will be informed of any changes <u>at the earliest opportunity</u>.
如果有任何改變，我們會在第一時間通知您。

例句❺ I've got <u>a window of opportunity</u> to talk to my boss about a pay rise tomorrow.
我明天有一個短暫的機會能和老闆談談加薪的事情。

實用短語 / 用法 / 句型

- at the earliest / first opportunity 在第一時間、盡快

- at every (available / possible) opportunity 一有機會

- the opportunity of a lifetime 一生一次的機會

- a window of opportunity 機會之窗、短暫的機會

- Opportunity knocks but once.
  大好的機會只會來一次，所以要好好把握。
  補充 < Don't miss the boat! > 別錯失機會了！

209

Option 選擇

▶ MP3-179

Adj. + option

attractive option	吸引人的選擇
preferred option	優先的選擇
available / feasible / viable option	可行的選擇
easy / soft option	輕鬆的選擇

V. + option

choose / exercise / select an option	選擇選項
specify an option	指定選項
favor an option	偏愛選項
assess / evaluate / weigh an option	評估、考量選項
list / outline an option	列出選項

例句❶ Solar energy could become a <u>viable option</u> for energy production.

太陽能可以成為能源生產的可行選項。

例句❷ We should <u>weigh the options</u> before we make a final decision.

我們應該先評估選項的利與弊再做最後決定。

例句❸ I'm <u>keeping my options open</u>, so I haven't signed the contract.

我會再考慮看看，暫時先不做決定，所以還沒有簽約。

實用短語 / 用法 / 句型

• have little / no option but to V. 別無選擇

• keep / leave one's options open 保留選擇暫時不做決定

Pain 疼痛、痛苦

▶ MP3-181

Adj. + pain

acute pain	急性的疼痛
chronic / nagging / persistent pain	長期的、持續的疼痛
burning / cramping / piercing / searing / shooting / stabbing / stinging / throbbing pain	刺痛、抽痛
agonizing / excruciating / intense / unbearable pain	劇烈難忍的疼痛
mild / moderate / slight pain	輕微的疼痛
dull pain	隱約的疼痛
intermittent pain	間歇性、斷斷續續的疼痛
indescribable / unspeakable pain	無法形容的痛苦

V. + pain

alleviate / decrease / dull / ease / lessen / reduce / relieve / soothe pain	減輕疼痛
eliminate pain	消除疼痛
aggravate / exacerbate / increase pain	加劇疼痛
cause / inflict pain	造成疼痛、痛苦

endure / put up with pain	忍受疼痛、痛苦
experience / go through pain	經歷疼痛、痛苦
heal pain	撫平傷痛
conceal / hide pain	隱藏傷痛
withstand pain	承受傷痛

pain + V.

pain flare up	疼痛復發
pain hit / strike + sb / sth	疼痛侵襲～
pain disappear / go / wear off	疼痛消退
pain persist	疼痛持續

▶ MP3-182

例句❶ Soon after injury, an ice bag can be applied to relieve pain and swelling.
剛受傷時，冰袋可用來減緩疼痛與腫脹。

例句❷ Through her drug addiction she had inflicted a lot of pain on the family.
由於吸毒的緣故，她造成了家人很大的痛苦。

例句❸ Nothing could heal the pain of her son's death.
任何事都無法撫平她的喪子之痛。

例句❹ Ben's ongoing foot pain flared up after he took a trip to Japan.
去日本旅行之後，Ben 的腳痛又復發了。

例句❺ A few hours after he'd had his tooth out, the pain began to wear off.

拔完牙幾小時後，他的疼痛開始消退。

例句❻ His face was contorted with pain as he crossed the finish line.

越過終點線時，他一臉痛苦。

例句❼ Ellen saw the pain etched on the man's face when he mentioned his ex-wife's name.

當這男人提到前妻的名字時，Ellen 看見了他臉上難過的表情。

例句❽ Your sister is a real pain in the neck. She's been playing that Rihanna song all afternoon.

你妹妹很令人頭痛，她整個下午不停地播蕾哈娜的歌曲。

實用短語 / 用法 / 句型

• aches and pains 疼痛

• discomfort and pain 身體不適和疼痛

• be racked with / suffer from pain 受疼痛折磨

• be contorted with pain 因痛苦扭曲變形

• the pain etched on sb's face 刻在臉上的痛苦

• cry out in / groan with / scream with pain 痛苦地喊叫

• on / under pain of sth 以～作威脅、違者以～論處

• a pain in the neck 令人頭痛的人或事、燙手山芋

Patience 耐心

▶ MP3-183

Adj. + patience

inexhaustible / unfailing / unlimited patience	無限的耐心

V. + patience

display / show patience	展現耐心
require / take patience	需要耐心
run out of patience	失去耐心
exhaust / stretch / tax sb's patience	耗盡耐心
test / try sb's patience	考驗耐心

patience + V.

patience run out / snap / wear out	耐心耗盡
patience wear thin	逐漸失去耐心、不耐煩

例句① He had been more annoying than usual and my patience was exhausted.

他比以往更煩人,我已經不耐煩了。

例句② Our patience is running out and we need you to make the final call.

我們快要沒耐心了,我們需要你來做最後的決定。

例句③ These endless meetings are enough to tax the patience of a saint.

就算是聖人,這些沒完沒了的會議也足以耗盡他的耐心。

實用短語 / 用法 / 句型

• the patience of a saint 如聖人般的耐心

Performance 表演、成果

▶ MP3-185

Adj. + performance

electrifying / impressive / stunning performance	驚艷的表現
dazzling performance	耀眼的表現
exceptional / extraordinary / outstanding / remarkable performance	卓越的表現
virtuoso performance	大師級的表現
strong / superb performance	極好的表現
satisfactory performance	令人滿意的表現
high performance	高效能
optimal performance	理想效能
mediocre performance	平庸的表現
disappointing / dismal / lackluster / poor performance	表現不佳
overall performance	整體的表現

V. + performance

deliver / give / produce a performance	演出、表現
put on / stage a performance	演出

補充 < put on a performance > 經常作
「裝腔作勢」、「偽裝演戲」的意思。

boost / improve a performance	提升表現
maximize / optimize a performance	最佳化表現
hinder a performance	妨礙表現
assess / evaluate performance	評估表現

▶ MP3-186

例句❶ The theater regularly puts on performances of Shakespeare and well known musicals.
這個劇場經常上演莎劇和知名的音樂劇。

例句❷ We provide expert support to extend the life of your systems and optimize their performance.
我們提供專業的技術支援，可以延長你們系統的壽命，也使系統能有最佳的表現。

例句❸ Supermarkets delivered a strong trading performance during the first half of the year.
超級市場的交易量在上半年度有強勁的表現。

Perspective 觀點、看法

▶ MP3-187

Adj. + perspective

alternative / contrasting / differing perspective	不同的觀點
broad / wide perspective	廣泛的觀點
narrow perspective	狹義的觀點
balanced perspective	平衡的觀點
holistic perspective	全面性的觀點
unique perspective	獨特的觀點
refreshing perspective	新穎的觀點

V. + perspective

embrace a perspective	抱持觀點
bring / offer / present / provide a perspective	提供觀點
adopt / take a perspective	採用觀點
shift a perspective	改變觀點
share a perspective	有相同的觀點
incorporate a perspective	納入觀點

例句❶ The film is made up of stories told by people with differing perspectives.

這部電影是由不同人的角度所述說的故事構成。

例句❷ This book presents a refreshing new perspective on a crucial period in our history.

這本書對一個歷史上重要的時期提出新觀點。

例句❸ There are allies who share our perspective and will work with us to secure common objectives.

有一些看法相同的同盟國會和我們並肩作戰,保衛共同的目標。

實用短語 / 用法 / 句型

• get / keep / place / put / see sth in perspective
  從宏觀、全面(性)的觀點看某事物

Phenomenon 現象

▶ MP3-189

Adj. + phenomenon

rare phenomenon	少見的現象
growing phenomenon	越來越普遍的現象
common / universal / widespread phenomenon	普遍的現象
bizarre / curious / mysterious / peculiar phenomenon	奇怪的現象
inexplicable phenomenon	無法解釋的現象
paranormal / supernatural phenomenon	超自然現象
natural phenomenon	自然的現象
emergent / recent phenomenon	新的現象

V. + phenomenon

investigate a phenomenon	調查現象
examine / observe / study a phenomenon	觀察、研究現象

phenomenon + V.

phenomenon arise / emerge / happen / occur	現象出現、發生

例句❶ Home education of children is a <u>growing phenomenon</u> in the UK.

兒童在家教育在英國是一個越來越普遍的現象。

例句❷ Racial hatred resulting in abuse and vicious murderous attacks is not a <u>recent phenomenon</u>.

造成虐待及蓄意攻擊的種族仇恨已經不是新現象了。

例句❸ <u>The phenomenon occurs</u> in the early stages of pregnancy.

這個現象發生在懷孕初期。

Policy 政策

Adj. + policy

deliberate policy	謹慎的政策
controversial policy	爭議性的政策
flawed / misguided policy	錯誤的政策
short-sighted policy	目光短淺的政策

V. + policy

draft / formulate / frame / make / plan policy	制訂政策
adopt / apply / carry out / implement / introduce policy	實施、採用政策
adhere to / follow policy	遵行政策
decide / determine / set policy	決定政策
amend / reverse / review / revise policy	修訂政策

policy + V.

policy is aimed at sth	政策針對～
policy govern sth	政策影響～
policy prohibit sth	政策禁止～

例句❶ We have to consider the benefits of the majority when formulating new policies.

在制訂政策時，我們必須考量多數人的利益。

例句❷ It would probably benefit all concerned to adopt a policy of cooperation.

採行合作政策可能會有益於所有相關的人。

例句❸ With the terrible traffic and high pollution, we must implement a strict policy.

有鑒於嚴重的交通與污染問題，我們必須實施嚴格的政策。

例句❹ It is a matter of company policy that we do not disclose the names of clients.

依公司的政策，我們不對外透露顧客的姓名。

實用短語 / 用法 / 句型

• a matter of policy 政策問題、事情

• policy wonk 政策專家（有癡迷的意味）

Potential 潛力、潛能

▶ MP3-193

Adj. + potential

considerable / enormous / immense / incredible / tremendous potential	很大的潛能
infinite / limitless / unlimited potential	無限的潛能
undoubted potential	無庸置疑的潛力
unfulfilled / untapped potential	未開發的潛能

V. + potential

demonstrate / show potential	展現潛能
achieve / fulfill / reach / realize potential	發揮潛力
exploit / harness / optimize / tap into / utilize potential	利用潛能
develop / unleash / unlock potential	開發潛能
identify / recognize / spot potential	找出、發現潛力

例句❶ We should be more innovative with our marketing, as there is great <u>untapped potential</u>.
我們必須更有創意，因為市場上有很多未開發的潛力。

例句❷ You should seize the opportunity to <u>demonstrate</u> your <u>potential</u>.
你要好好把握這個機會展現潛力。

例句❸ Our aim is to ensure that every student <u>realizes</u> his or her full <u>potential</u>.
我們的目標是確保每個學生都能充分發揮潛力。

Progress 進步、進展

▶ MP3-195

Adj. + progress

gradual / incremental / smooth / steady progress	逐漸的進展
rapid / speedy / swift progress	迅速的進展
considerable / enormous / remarkable / significant / substantial / tremendous progress	重大的進展
genuine progress	真正的進展
solid progress	穩固的進展
continued / sustained progress	持續的進展
further progress	進一步的進展

V. + progress

achieve / make progress	達到進展、進步
chart / follow / monitor / track progress	追蹤、監控進展
accelerate / facilitate progress	加速進展
delay / hamper / hinder / hold back / impede / inhibit / obstruct progress	阻礙進展
arrest / block / halt progress	遏止、終止進展
assess / evaluate / gauge / measure progress	評估進展

| check (on) / review progress | 檢視進展 |
| mark progress | 顯示進展 |

▶ MP3-196

例句① We have <u>made significant progress</u> in the fight against AIDS.
我們在對抗愛滋病上已經有了重大的進展。

例句② The latest sales figures <u>mark the continued progress</u> of the business.
最新的銷售數字顯示公司的持續進展。

例句③ They will use the new camera to <u>chart the progress</u> of building works currently being carried out at the school.
他們將利用新的攝影機監控學校建築工程的進展。

例句④ <u>Progress was impeded</u> by problems of access and planning permission.
進度因使用權及規劃許可證的問題受阻。

例句⑤ The development and definition of a brand is always, to a certain extent, <u>work in progress</u>.
品牌發展和品牌定義某種程度上來說，沒有完美的一天。

實用短語 / 用法 / 句型

- work in progress 半成品、施工中
- in progress 進行中

Purpose 目的、用途

Adj. + purpose

chief / main / primary purpose	主要的目的
particular / special / specific purpose	特定的目的
common / shared purpose	共同的目的
general purpose	一般的目的
original purpose	最初的目的
sole purpose	唯一的目的
practical / useful purpose	實際的用途
dual purpose	雙重的用途
intended purpose	預期的目的

V. + purpose

accomplish / achieve / fulfill a purpose	達成目的
answer / meet / serve a purpose	有利於達成目的
defeat a purpose	使目的失敗、無意義
suit a purpose	符合目的
account for a purpose	解釋目的
outline a purpose	敘述、表明目的

例句❶ The <u>original purpose</u> of the experiment was to study the effects of physical conditions on productivity.

這個實驗最初的目的是研究身體狀況對生產力的影響。

例句❷ These small village shops <u>serve</u> a very <u>useful purpose</u>.

村莊裡的這幾間小商店對居民生活很有幫助。

例句❸ The questionnaires clearly <u>outlined the purpose</u> of the exercise.

問卷清楚解釋了這個練習的目的。

例句❹ I think we've been talking <u>at cross purposes</u>. I meant last year, not next year.

我覺得我們在講不同的東西。我指的是去年，不是明年。

例句❺ They painted the house <u>for the express purpose of</u> selling it .

他們特別為了賣房而漆房子。

例句❻ Either method you use will, <u>for all practical purposes</u>, have the same result.

事實上，這兩種方法都會得到一樣的結果。

實用短語 / 用法 / 句型

• at cross purposes 有不同的目標、無共識、在講不同的東西

• for / with the express purpose of sth 特別為了～目的

• for (all) practical purposes 實際上、實質上

• one's purpose in life 生活、人生的目的

• a sense of purpose 使命感

• strength of purpose 決心

• on purpose 故意地

Question 問題、待討論的問題、疑問 ▶ MP3-199

Adj. + question

intriguing question	有趣的問題
challenging / thorny / tough / tricky question	難回答的、棘手的問題
pointed / probing / searching question	深入尖銳的問題
direct / straight question	直接的問題
open-ended question	開放性的問題
hypothetical question	假設性的問題
leading / loaded / trick question	誘導性的問題
pertinent / relevant question	和主題相關的問題
basic / fundamental question	基本的問題
quick question	小問題（很快地問一下）
outstanding / unanswered / unresolved question	未解決的問題
burning question	亟待解決的問題
critical / crucial / major / vital question	重要的問題
controversial / vexed question	爭議性的問題

V. + question

bring up / pose / put / raise a question	提出問題
bombard sb with questions	向某人連續提出問題
fire / shoot questions at sb	向某人連續提出問題
reply to / respond to a question	回答問題
dodge / evade / ignore / parry / sidestep a question	閃避問題
formulate / frame / phrase a question	表達、闡述問題
rephrase a question	用不同方式表達問題
address / confront / handle / face / tackle a question	面對、處理問題
field questions	回答一連串的問題
explore a question	探討問題
come into question	成為待討論的問題
be open to question	有待爭論
call into question	對～感到懷疑

question + V.

question arise	問題出現

例句❶ He became embarrassed when a journalist asked him <u>pointed questions</u> about his affair.

當記者對緋聞提出尖銳問題時，他變得有些尷尬。

例句❷ I have a <u>quick question</u>. When is the application deadline?

我有一個小問題，請問申請截止日是什麼時候？

例句❸ It is a <u>burning question</u> whether we should maintain the current administrative system or not.

是否該維持現行的行政制度是一個亟待解決的問題。

例句❹ A reporter <u>bombarded</u> the president <u>with questions</u> about his economic policy.

記者對總統的經濟政策提出一連串問題。

例句❺ In an investigation of this type, you need to take great care in the way you <u>frame</u> your <u>questions</u>.

在這種類型的調查中，你必須要注意自己表達問題的方式。

例句❻ After the break, Robinson <u>fielded questions</u> on his career.

在休息過後，Robinson 回答了關於自己職業生涯的種種問題。

例句❼ It does <u>call into question</u> the decision to send troops into the area.

派遣軍隊進入該地區的這個決定確實使民眾感到懷疑。

例句❽ A trip to New Zealand is <u>out of the question</u> this year.

今年是不可能去紐西蘭旅遊。

實用短語 / 用法 / 句型

• out of the question 不可能

• out of question 無庸置疑

Realm 領域、範圍、領土

▶ MP3-201

Adj. + realm

public realm	公共領域、空間
private realm	私人領域

V. + realm

belong to the realm	屬於～領域
lie in the realm	位於～領域
open up a realm	開啟（新）方向、開發新範疇
enter / move into a realm	進入領域
defend a realm	保衛領土

▶ MP3-202

例句❶ The late debate has spilled over into the public realm.
不久前的爭論已經擴大到公共領域。

例句❷ The research has opened up new realms for investigation.
這份研究為調查工作開啟新的範疇。

例句❸ It's not beyond the realm of possibility that some companies may have to cut back on staff.
可能會有一些公司必須削減員工的數量。

實用短語 / 用法 / 句型

• within the realms of possibility 有可能
• beyond the realms of possibility 不可能

Recognition 認識、辨認、承認、讚譽

▶ MP3-203

Adj. + recognition

instant recognition	即時的辨認
early recognition	早期、及時的辨別
clear / explicit recognition	明確的認識
general / universal recognition	普遍的認識、認同
increasing / growing recognition	逐漸認識到、承認
due / well-deserved recognition	應有的認同
tacit recognition	默認
full recognition	全面的認可
mutual recognition	相互承認
formal / official recognition	正式的、官方的認可
international recognition	國際的認同
de facto recognition	實質上的承認

V. + recognition

show recognition	表示認識
avoid recognition	避免被認出
achieve / obtain / receive / win recognition	獲得認同、讚譽
earn sb recognition	為某人贏得認同、讚譽

deserve / merit recognition	值得認同、讚許
ask for / call for / seek recognition	尋求認同、認可
confer recognition (+ on sth)	給予認同、讚許
give / grant + sb / sth recognition	認同、讚許～
deny / refuse + sb / sth recognition	不予認同、不承認

recognition + V.

| recognition come | 得到認可 |

▶ MP3-204

例句❶ Early recognition of a disease and appropriate treatment is important for patients.
及早發現疾病並給予適當治療對病人很重要。

例句❷ There's a growing recognition that this country can no longer afford the health insurance system.
民眾逐漸意識到，這個國家再也無法負擔健保制度。

例句❸ This promotion is a well-deserved recognition for his achievements.
這次升遷是對他的成就一個應有的肯定。

例句❹ His recitals have earned him recognition as a talented performer.
他的獨奏會為他贏得天才演奏家的美譽。

例句❺ We have an honors system designed precisely to confer public recognition on acts of personal good.
我們有一個獎勵制度來表揚個人善行。

例句❻ She stared at the man without a flicker of recognition.
她一臉不認識的樣子盯著那個男人。

例句❼ The societal recognition of the importance of historical culture is becoming increasingly popular.
歷史文化的重要性越來越受到社會重視。

例句❽ When he returned to his home town after the war, he found it had changed out of all recognition.
當他在戰爭結束後回到家鄉，才發現一切都已經面目全非。

實用短語 / 用法 / 句型

- a flicker / sign of recognition 一點點的認識

- recognition of the importance of sth 認識到、承認～的重要性

- recognition of the need for sth 認識到、承認～的必要性

- a struggle for recognition 爭取認同

- out of all recognition (= beyond recognition) 面目全非、認不得

Reform 改良、改革、改過

Adj. + reform

drastic / fundamental / radical reform	徹底的改革
far-reaching / sweeping / wide-ranging reform	全面的改革
significant reform	重大的改革
piecemeal reform	零星的、逐步的改革
rapid reform	快速的改革
lasting reform	持續的改革
(long) overdue reform	遲來的、早該要有的改革
fiscal reform	財政改革
curriculum reform	課綱改革
pension reform	年金改革

V. + reform

advocate / back / embrace / favor a reform	主張、支持改革
press for / push for a reform	迫切要求改革
enact / implement / introduce / undertake a reform	進行、實施改革

carry out / drive through / push through a reform	進行、實施改革
bring about a reform	造成改革
accelerate a reform	加速改革
block / delay a reform	阻礙改革
require reform	需要改革

reform + V.

| reform go through | 改革通過 |
| reform fail | 改革失敗 |

▶ MP3-206

例句❶ The Prime Minister promised <u>sweeping reforms</u> of the banking system.
首相承諾銀行體制將進行全面改革。

例句❷ Markets are already losing confidence in <u>piecemeal reform</u>.
市場對於零星的改革已經失去信心。

例句❸ They have issued a statement <u>advocating reform</u> of the legal system.
他們發表了一份聲明，主張改革法律制度。

例句❹ They wanted to <u>push through radical reforms</u>.
他們想要進行徹底的改革。

例句❺ <u>The reforms went through</u> in spite of opposition from teachers.
儘管老師反對，改革還是通過了。

實用短語 / 用法 / 句型

- a package of reforms 一套改革方案

- the need for reform 改革的需要

- the pace of reform 改革的步伐

- a program of reform (= a reform program) 改革計畫

Relationship 關聯、關係、人際關係

▶ MP3-207

Adj. + relationship

causal relationship	因果關係
close relationship	密切的關係
complex / complicated relationship	複雜的關係
inverse / negative relationship	相反的、反向的關係
intimate relationship	親密的關係
lasting / long-standing relationship	長久的關係
stable / steady relationship	穩定的關係
rocky / stormy / volatile relationship	不穩定的關係
troubled relationship	麻煩的、緊張的關係

V. + relationship

build / develop / establish / forge / foster / strike up a relationship	建立、培養關係
cement / strengthen a relationship	加強、鞏固關係
maintain a relationship	維持關係
repair a relationship	修復關係
ruin / undermine a relationship	破壞關係
break off a relationship	斷絕關係

relationship + V.

relationship emerge	顯示出～關係
relationship evolve / progress	關係進展、發展
relationship break down / break up / fail	關係破裂

▶ MP3-208

例句❶ The study shows the inverse relationship between email volume and response rates.
這份研究顯示出電子郵件數量與回覆速度的反向關係。

例句❷ My boyfriend and I have had a rocky relationship since we moved in together.
自從我和男朋友住在一起，我們的關係就不太穩定。

例句❸ By forging strong relationships with private landowners and environmental organizations, the company has an advantage over others.
藉由與私有地主及環保機構打好關係，這間公司比其他公司來的有優勢。

例句❹ An atmosphere of suspicion can ruin relationships and undermine confidence.
相互猜疑的氛圍會破壞彼此的關係，同時也會削弱信心。

例句❺ A clear relationship emerged in the study between happiness and level of education.
這份研究顯示出幸福和教育程度之間的明顯關係。

實用短語 / 用法 / 句型

- the breakdown of a relationship (= relationship breakdown)
  關係破裂

- the nature of the relationship 關係的本質

Remark 言論、評論

▶ MP3-209

Adj. + remark

opening remark	開場白
closing / concluding remark	結語
casual / chance / off-the-cuff / throwaway remark	即興的、不經意的談論
brief / passing remark	簡短的評論
caustic / cutting / pointed / scathing / snide remark	尖刻的評論
defamatory / derogatory / disparaging / insulting / offensive remark	侮辱的、冒犯的評論
crude / rude remark	無理的言論
sarcastic remark	諷刺的評論
flippant / offhand remark	輕率的、不假思索的言論
tongue-in-cheek remark	半開玩笑不可當真的言論
facetious / witty remark	幽默風趣的言論
complimentary remark	讚美的、恭維的評論
flattering remark	奉承的言論
inflammatory / provocative remark	挑釁的言論

V. + remark

deliver / make / pass a remark	做出評論
withdraw a remark	收回、撤回評論

remark + V.

remark be directed at sb	評論針對某人
remark provoke sth	言論激起、引發某事
remark reflect sth	言論反映某事

▶ MP3-210

例句❶ I'm surprised this caused such a result, as it was just a throwaway remark.
我很意外這會造成這樣的結果,因為我當初只是隨口說說罷了。

例句❷ Let me conclude with some passing remarks about the country's defence industry.
讓我針對這個國家的國防工業做簡短的評論以作為總結。

例句❸ He made some snide remarks at his opponent's competence.
他對對手的能力做出刻薄的評論。

例句❹ He was expelled from the party for failing to withdraw his controversial remarks.
他因為未能收回具爭議的言論而被開除黨籍。

例句❺ The remark provoked an outcry from the crowd.
這番言論激起了眾怒。

Reputation 名聲、聲望

▶ MP3-211

Adj. + reputation

impressive / solid / strong reputation	良好的聲望、美譽
legendary / outstanding / stellar / sterling / unrivalled reputation	卓越的聲望
well-deserved / well-earned reputation	應有的聲望
long-established / long-standing / well-established reputation	悠久的名聲
burgeoning / growing reputation	上升的聲望
fearsome reputation	令人生畏的名聲
world-class reputation	世界級的美譽
dubious / questionable reputation	有疑慮的名聲
tainted / tarnished reputation	受損的聲譽
infamous / notorious reputation	臭名、聲名狼藉

V. + reputation

boast / enjoy / have / hold a reputation	享有名聲
build / carve (out) / create / develop / establish a reputation	建立聲望
achieve / acquire / earn / gain / garner / win a reputation	獲得名聲

cement / confirm / consolidate / reinforce / uphold a reputation	鞏固名聲
boost / enhance / improve a reputation	提升聲望
deserve / live up to a reputation	無愧於名聲、名副其實
damage / destroy / harm / ruin / sully / tarnish a reputation	損害、玷污名聲
compromise / risk / stake a reputation	危及名聲
defend / preserve / protect a reputation	維護名聲
maintain / retain a reputation	保持名聲
save a reputation	挽救聲望
restore a reputation	恢復聲望
shed a reputation	擺脫名聲

reputation + V.

reputation suffer	名聲受損、受創
reputation depend on / rest on sth	名聲取決於、依靠某事

▶ MP3-212

例句❶ America is struggling to <u>restore</u> its <u>tarnished reputation</u>.
美國正努力恢復它受損的聲譽。

例句❷ The company has <u>built</u> an enviable <u>reputation</u> based on service and quality.
因為良好的服務與品質，該公司已經建立了令人稱羨的聲譽。

例句❸ Her international <u>reputation is carved out</u> by an impressive list of publications.

一系列令人印象深刻的出版品使她的名聲享譽國際。

例句❹ As a Michelin-starred restaurant, Din Tai Fung <u>lives up to</u> its <u>reputation</u>.

作為米其林一星的餐廳，鼎泰豐果然名副其實。

例句❺ The country has definitively <u>shed</u> its <u>reputation</u> for economic mismanagement.

這個國家最後已經擺脫了經濟管理不善的名聲。

例句❻ The company's <u>reputation suffered</u> when it had to recall thousands of products.

當公司不得不召回成千上萬的產品時，公司的聲譽已經受創。

例句❼ She was willing to <u>put her reputation on the line</u> in order to get political progress.

為了使政治能有所進步，她願意賭上自己的名聲。

例句❽ We knew him before the meeting because <u>his reputation</u> had already <u>preceded him</u>.

他的聲名遠播，在見面之前我們就知道他了。

實用短語 / 用法 / 句型

- put one's reputation on the line
  賭上某人名聲、冒著賠上某人名聲的危險

- sb's reputation precedes sb
  某人的名聲走在前面（= 聲名遠播，可以是好的名聲也可以是不好的）

Resource 資源

Adj. + resource

finite / limited resources	有限的資源
meager / scarce resources	貧乏的資源
dwindling resources	逐漸減少的資源
abundant / considerable / enormous / extensive / rich / substantial / vast resources	大量的資源
adequate / sufficient resources	足夠的資源
vital resources	重要的資源
renewable / sustainable resources	可再生的、永續的資源
untapped resources	未開發的資源
human resources	人力資源

V. + resource

allocate / commit / distribute resources (+ to sth)	分配資源
divert resources	挪用、轉移資源
devote resources (+ to sth)	把資源用於～
pour resources (+ into sth)	投入資源
deploy / draw on / exploit / tap (into) / utilize resources	使用、利用資源

consume / expend resources	花費資源
deplete / drain / exhaust / use up resources	耗盡資源
pool / share resources	集結、共享資源
conserve resources	保存資源

▶ MP3-214

例句❶ Air pollution, endangered species, polluted oceans, and dwinding natural resources are important issues we face today.
空氣污染、瀕危的物種、海洋污染、逐漸匱乏的自然資源是我們當今所面臨的重要議題。

例句❷ Central government is failing to allocate adequate financial resources to the social care sector.
中央政府未能分配足夠的財政資源給社會福利部門。

例句❸ Companies that wish to achieve sustainable success must commit sufficient resources to research and development.
公司若想要持續成功，就必須分配足夠的資源給研發部門。

例句❹ All students are encouraged to utilize the center's resources for study and research.
學校鼓勵學生利用中心的資源學習和研究。

例句❺ The Olympics may deplete the country's resources.
奧運可能會耗盡這個國家的所有資源。

例句❻ There are hundreds of tools and resources at your disposal.
你有上百種的工具和資源可以使用。

實用短語 / 用法 / 句型

- resource allocation 資源分配

- resource exploitation 資源利用

- the resources at sb's disposal 可供某人使用的資源

- time and resources 時間和資源

Response 答覆、反應

Adj. + response

encouraging / enthusiastic / favorable / positive response	熱情的、正向的回應
affirmative response	肯定的答覆
prompt / quick / speedy / swift response	立即的、快速的反應
adequate / appropriate / proper response	適當的回應
timely response	及時的回應
strong response	強烈的回應
negative response	負面的回應
lukewarm / muted / tepid response	不熱烈的、冷淡的回應
delayed response	遲來的回應
brusque / curt response	唐突、草率的回應
instinctive / knee-jerk response	本能的、下意識的反應
written response	書面的回應
initial response	最初的反應

V. + response

attract / bring / call forth / draw / elicit / evoke / generate / induce / prompt / provoke / trigger a response	造成、引起反應

receive a response	得到回應
formulate a response	做出回應
exhibit / show a response	呈現、顯現反應
gauge a response	評估反應

▶ MP3-216

例句❶ The piece <u>receives an enthusiastic response</u> from the audience.
這個作品獲得觀眾熱烈的回應。

例句❷ Her proposal got a <u>lukewarm response</u> from the board.
她的提案得到了董事會冷淡的回應。

例句❸ When an earthquake strikes, my <u>instinctive response</u> is to run.
地震發生時，我本能的反應就是往外跑。

例句❹ His comments <u>prompted</u> an angry <u>response</u> from environmentalists.
他的言論激怒了環保人士。

例句❺ We sent out over 100 letters but the <u>response rate</u> was low.
我們寄出了超過 100 封信，但回覆率卻很低。

實用短語 / 用法 / 句型

• response rate 反應率、回覆率

Responsibility 責任、責任感 ▶ MP3-217

Adj. + responsibility

complete / full / overall / total responsibility	全部的、全權的責任
ultimate responsibility	最終的、完全的責任
primary / prime responsibility	主要的責任
sole responsibility	唯一的、單獨的責任
awesome / enormous / grave / heavy / huge / tremendous / weighty responsibility	重大的責任
onerous responsibility	繁重的責任
collective / joint / mutual / shared responsibility	共同的、連帶責任
legal responsibility	法律上的責任
parental responsibility	父母的責任
corporate response	企業責任

V. + responsibility

accept / assume / bear / shoulder / take (on) / undertake responsibility	承擔責任
take over responsibility	接管責任
carry out / discharge / fulfill / meet responsibilities	履行責任

share responsibility	分擔責任
admit / claim responsibility	承認責任、宣稱對某事負責
feel a responsibility	覺得有責任
assign / delegate responsibility (+ to sb)	委派、指派責任
hand over / pass / transfer responsibility (+ to sb)	移交責任
devolve responsibility (+ on / upon sb)	移交責任
charge sb with responsibility	託付某人責任
lay / place responsibility for sth on sb	將某事交予某人負責
retain responsibility	保留、保有責任
abdicate responsibility	放棄責任
deny / disclaim responsibility	拒絕承擔責任
duck / escape / evade / shirk / shrink from responsibility	逃避責任
shift responsibility (+ onto sb)	推卸責任
attribute responsibility to sb	將責任歸咎於某人
burden sb with responsibility	使某人背負責任
absolve sb from / of responsibility	免除某人～的責任

responsibility + V.

responsibility fall on / lie with / rest with sb	責任落在某人身上

例句① The committee <u>takes overall responsibility</u> for finance and budgeting.
委員會全權負責財務與編列預算。

例句② We will <u>shoulder</u> our <u>responsibility</u> and accept the deserved punishment.
我們會承擔責任並接受應有的處分。

例句③ No organization has yet <u>claimed responsibility</u> for the bomb attack.
目前還沒有組織宣稱這起炸彈攻擊為其所為。

例句④ To be a good manager, you must know how to <u>devolve responsibility</u> downwards.
要當一位好的經理，你必須要知道如何下放責任。

例句⑤ They wanted to <u>shift responsibility</u> for the failure <u>onto</u> their employees.
他們想將失敗的責任推到員工身上。

例句⑥ The responsibility for the disaster has <u>been laid at the company's door</u>.
這場大禍的罪責全在公司。

例句⑦ I feel I am in <u>a position of responsibility</u> for this project.
我覺得我在這個計畫中肩負責任。

實用短語 / 用法 / 句型

• a burden of responsibility 責任的重擔

• lay the responsibility (fairly and squarely) at sb's door 責任歸咎於某人

• a position of responsibility 擔負責任的職位

• a feeling / sense of responsibility 責任感

• corporate social responsibility (= CSR) 社會企業責任

Restriction 限制

Adj. + restriction

draconian / harsh / severe / strict / stringent / strong / tight / tough restriction	嚴格的限制
arbitrary restriction	武斷的限制
undue restriction	過度的限制
unnecessary / unreasonable restriction	不必要的、不合理的限制
self-imposed restriction	自我的限制、約束
legal / legislative / statutory restriction	法律限制、法規限制
dietary restriction	飲食限制
security restriction	安全限制
smoking restriction	禁菸限制

V. + restriction

enforce / impose / place / put restrictions (+ on)	實施、施加限制
apply restrictions (+ to)	施加限制
introduce restrictions	引入限制
comply with / meet / observe restrictions	遵守、符合限制
abolish / ease / lift / remove restrictions	解除限制

loosen restrictions   放鬆、放寬限制

breach / violate restrictions 違反限制

bypass / circumvent restrictions 規避限制

be subject to restrictions   受限制影響

restriction + V.

restrictions apply   限制適用

▶ MP3-220

例句❶ We would have to impose much tighter restrictions on motoring, but this is politically risky.
我們必須對汽車實施更嚴格的限制，但這有政治風險。

例句❷ We urge members to resist arbitrary restrictions placed upon their activities.
我們勸成員抵制活動上武斷的限制。

例句❸ The major supermarkets wanted the Government to lift all restrictions on trading.
超市龍頭希望政府能解除交易上的所有限制。

例句❹ Confidentiality restrictions prevent me from giving any names.
保密限制禁止我說出任何名字。

Routine 例行公事、慣例

Adj. + routine

daily / day-to-day routine	例行公事、慣例
dreary / dull / humdrum / monotonous / predictable / repetitive routine	單調乏味的例行公事
hectic routine	繁忙的例行公事

V. + routine

establish / fall into / get into / settle into a routine	建立慣例、養成習慣
get stuck in a routine	陷為例行公事
follow / go through a routine	遵從慣例、進行例行公事
break / change a routine	打破、改變慣例
disrupt / disturb / interrupt / upset a routine	擾亂例行公事

例句❶ She wants to escape from the <u>monotonous routine</u> of work.
她想擺脫單調乏味的日常工作。

例句❷ She is <u>settling into the hectic routine</u> of having a new-born baby.
她習慣了有新生兒的繁忙日常生活。

例句❸ You should help your toddler learn to go to bed by <u>establishing</u> a bedtime <u>routine</u>.
你應該幫助你的孩子養成就寢習慣，要他在固定的時間上床睡覺。

例句❹ The building work will inevitably <u>disrupt</u> the normal <u>routines</u> of the office.
建築工程必定會擾亂正常的例行工作。

例句❺ Bags of all visitors to the museum are searched as <u>a matter of routine</u>.
參觀博物館民眾的背包都會照常規被檢查。

實用短語 / 用法 / 句型

- a change from / in / of the routine 常規的改變

- a matter of routine 常規、例行公事

- routine chore 日常家務

- routine task 例行任務

- routine check / check-up / examination / inspection 例行檢查

- routine cleaning 例行清潔工作

- routine maintenance 例行維護

- routine follow-up 例行回診

- routine patrol 例行巡邏

- routine immunization / vaccination 例行疫苗接種

Satisfaction 滿意、愉快　　　▶ MP3-223

Adj. + satisfaction

considerable / deep / high / immense / ultimate satisfaction	非常滿意
complete / full / total satisfaction	完全滿意
little / low satisfaction	不滿意、滿意度低
general / overall satisfaction	總體滿意度
smug satisfaction	沾沾自喜、自鳴得意
mutual satisfaction	相互滿意

V. + satisfaction

achieve / experience / feel / find satisfaction	達到滿意、獲得滿足
derive / gain / get / take satisfaction	獲得滿足
express / indicate / show satisfaction	表示滿意
afford / bring / provide satisfaction	提供滿意、滿足
assure / ensure / guarantee satisfaction	保證滿意
assess / gauge / measure satisfaction	評估滿意度
enhance / improve / increase satisfaction	提升滿意度
seek satisfaction	尋求滿足感

例句❶ He has <u>derived immense satisfaction</u> from teaching English to children in rural areas.
他從教導鄉下孩童英語的過程中獲得很大的成就感。

例句❷ There was a hint of <u>smug self-satisfaction</u> in her voice.
她的聲音中帶有一絲絲得意。

例句❸ Every part of the book would <u>afford satisfaction</u> and information to its readers.
這本書的每一部分都提供讀者資訊，也為讀者帶來滿足。

例句❹ The questionnaire is designed to <u>measure</u> the job <u>satisfaction</u> or dissatisfaction of teachers.
這份問卷用來測量老師對工作滿意或不滿意。

例句❺ <u>To my</u> great <u>satisfaction</u>, my assumption was proved right.
令我滿意的是，我的假定被證實是對的。

實用短語 / 用法 / 句型

• a certain satisfaction 某種程度的滿意

• a grin / smile / smirk of satisfaction 滿意的笑容

• a look of satisfaction 滿意的表情

• a feeling / sense of satisfaction 滿足感

• a source of satisfaction 滿意、滿足的來源

• service satisfaction 服務滿意度

• client / customer satisfaction 顧客滿意度

• to one's satisfaction 令某人感到滿意

Scandal 醜聞

▶ MP3-225

Adj. + scandal

big / huge / major / real scandal	大醜聞
minor scandal	小醜聞
high-profile / notorious / public / tabloid scandal	眾所矚目的醜聞
alleged scandal	聲稱但未經證實的醜聞
juicy / sensational scandal	引起轟動的醜聞

V. + scandal

expose / reveal / uncover a scandal	揭發醜聞
bring / cause / lead to a scandal	造成醜聞
be embroiled in / be implicated in / be involved in a scandal	身陷醜聞
cover up / hush up a scandal	掩蓋醜聞

scandal + V.

scandal break / ensue / erupt / unfold	爆發醜聞
scandal dog / engulf / hit / surround + sb / sth	醜聞困擾～
scandal rock / shake + sb / sth	醜聞動搖～
scandal die down	醜聞逐漸消失

例句❶ He made many enemies and seemed to be dogged by minor scandals.
他與許多人交惡，似乎還身受一些小醜聞的困擾。

例句❷ The scandal was uncovered by The New York Times.
這起醜聞被紐約時報揭發。

例句❸ He was embroiled in a scandal that effectively ended his political career.
他身陷一起醜聞，而這起醜聞結束了他的政治生涯。

例句❹ The scandal unfolded at the end of December.
這起醜聞在十二月底爆發。

例句❺ The government was rocked by a series of scandals.
政府被接二連三的醜聞影響。

例句❻ Until the story was published there had been no hint of scandal.
在新聞被報導出來前都沒有一絲醜聞的跡象。

實用短語 / 用法 / 句型

- bribery scandal 行賄醜聞
- corruption scandal 貪污醜聞
- match-fixing scandal 假球醜聞
- sexual scandal 性醜聞
- a series / spate / wave of scandals 接二連三的醜聞
- the center of a scandal 醜聞的焦點
- a breath / hint / suggestion of scandal 一絲絲醜聞的跡象
- in the wake of a scandal 繼醜聞之後

Schedule 時間表、行程表

▶ MP3-227

Adj. + schedule

busy / crowded / demanding / exhausting / gruelling / hectic / packed / punishing / rigorous / strict / tight schedule	繁忙的行程表
flexible schedule	有彈性的行程表
fixed schedule	固定的時間表
rotating schedule	輪班制的時間表

V. + schedule

arrange / draw up / plan / prepare / set / work out a schedule	規劃行程表
adjust / revise / update a schedule	更改行程表
adhere to / conform to / keep to / meet / stay on / stick to / work to a schedule	按照行程表做事
take time out of a schedule	抽空、抽出時間
fit sth into a schedule	將某事排入行程

例句❶ Some presenters, feeling the strain of a <u>hectic</u> television <u>schedule</u>, might practice yoga to relax.

一些因為忙碌的電視節目行程而倍感壓力的主持人，可能會透過做瑜伽放鬆一下。

例句❷ We had to work a lot of overtime to <u>stay on the strict</u> production <u>schedule</u>.

我們必須時常加班來趕上嚴格的生產進度。

例句❸ Thank you for <u>taking time out of</u> your busy <u>schedule</u> to visit our school.

謝謝你在百忙之中抽空拜訪我們學校。

例句❹ After weeks of bad weather, the construction project <u>is</u> seriously <u>behind schedule</u>.

在幾個禮拜的壞天氣之後，建設工程的進度嚴重落後。

實用短語 / 用法 / 句型

• be ahead of / run ahead of schedule 進度、行程超前

• be behind / fall behind schedule 進度、行程落後

Stance 位置、立場、態度

▶ MP3-229

Adj. + stance

adversarial / aggressive / confrontational / defensive / defiant / oppositional stance	對立的立場
hardline / hawkish / rigid / tough / uncompromising / unwavering stance	強硬的、不妥協的立場
firm / purposeful / strong stance	堅定的態度
proactive stance	積極的態度
radical stance	激進的態度
cautious stance	謹慎的態度
neutral stance	中立的態度
principled stance	根據原則所採取的立場
anti-war stance	反戰的立場

V. + stance

adopt / assume / take a stance	採取立場
maintain a stance	維持、保持立場
abandon a stance	放棄立場
alter / change / modify / reverse / shift a stance	改變立場
affirm / clarify / uphold a stance	申明、確認立場

reiterate a stance	重申立場
harden / toughen a stance	強化、堅定立場
loosen / moderate / relax / soften a stance	軟化立場
compromise / contradict / undermine / weaken a stance	削弱立場
justify a stance	合理化立場
applaud / back / endorse a stance	支持、贊同立場
defend a stance	捍衛立場
criticize / deplore a stance	批評立場
oppose / question a stance	反對立場

▶ MP3-230

例句❶ We took a clear and uncompromising stance against collaboration with our persecutors.
我們採取明確且強硬的立場，拒絕與迫害者合作。

例句❷ Lawmakers should take a proactive stance to protect these animals.
立法者應該採取積極主動的態度保護這些動物。

例句❸ Experts are urging the government to shift its stance on cannabis.
專家力勸政府改變其對大麻的態度。

例句❹ We believe that the local authority needs to toughen its stance and focus more on enforcement.
我們認為地方政府需要堅定其立場並更專注在執行上。

例句❺ Customers have questioned the company's ethical stance.
顧客已經在質疑公司的道德態度了。

Standard 標準、水準

▶ MP3-231

Adj. + standard

exacting / strict / stringent / tough standard	嚴格的標準
acceptable / decent / reasonable / satisfactory standard	尚可接受的標準
mandatory / recommended / required standard	規定的、要求的標準
minimum standard	最低標準
accepted / agreed / appropriate / approved / common / consistent / harmonized / recognized standard	共同的、一致的標準
current standard	現行標準
improved / rising standard	提高的標準
declining / falling standard	下降的標準
double standard	雙重標準
living standard	生活水平

V. + standard

define / develop / establish / lay down / set a standard	建立、制訂標準
adopt a standard	採用標準
propose a standard	提出標準
achieve / attain / comply with / conform to / live up to / match / meet / reach / satisfy a standard	達到、符合標準
exceed / surpass a standard	超越、超過標準
fall short of a standard	未達標準
keep to / maintain / uphold a standard	維持標準
improve / raise standards	提升水準
compromise / lower standards	降低水準
apply / enforce / implement / impose a standard	實施標準

例句① We will work on your vehicle until it <u>meets</u> our <u>exacting standards</u>.
我們將會處理你的車子，直到它符合我們嚴格的標準為止。

例句② They will <u>adopt common standards</u> for dealing with asylum applications.
他們將採用一致的標準來處理避難申請。

例句③ Companies have been expelled from membership for failing to <u>meet the standards required</u>.
許多公司因為沒有達到規定的標準，已經被開除會員資格了。

例句④ All our products far <u>exceed</u> the appropriate safety <u>standards</u>, giving you added peace of mind.
我們所有的產品都遠遠超越適當的安全標準，讓您更加安心。

例句⑤ The Environment Agency <u>enforces strict</u> water quality <u>standards</u>.
環保局施行嚴格的水質標準。

例句⑥ The army was massive <u>by the standards of the day</u>.
從現代的標準來看，這支軍隊的規模相當龐大。

實用短語 / 用法 / 句型

- by any standard 以任何標準來看
- by the standards of the day 以現今的標準來看
- a drop / fall in the standard 標準的下降
- an increase / a rise in the standard 標準的上升
- a standard of living (= living standards) 生活水平
- standards of behavior (= standards of conduct) 行為標準

Strategy 策略、對策

▶ MP3-233

Adj. + strategy

overall / overarching strategy	總體的策略
forward / long-term strategy	未來的、長期的策略
cost-effective strategy	符合成本效益的策略
practical / viable strategy	可行的策略
sensible strategy	明智的策略
effective / proven / robust / sound strategy	有效的、健全的策略
optimal strategy	最佳的策略
winning strategy	成功的、致勝的策略
alternative strategy	不同的策略
integrated strategy	整合的、綜合的策略
ambitious / grand strategy	有雄心的、偉大的策略
high-risk / risky strategy	有風險的、危險的策略
proactive strategy	積極主動的策略
deliberate strategy	深思熟慮的、蓄意的策略
dual / two-pronged strategy	雙重策略
market-oriented strategy	市場導向的策略
coping strategy	應對策略

V. + strategy

arrive at / come up with / design / develop / devise / establish / formulate / map out / plan / produce / work out a strategy	想出、策劃策略
define / draw up / outline / set out a strategy	草擬、制定策略
agree on / decide on / negotiate a strategy	同意、決定策略
assess / consider / evaluate / examine / look at a strategy	評估、考量策略
adopt / apply / embark on / employ / execute / implement / launch / pursue / utilize a strategy	採取、運用策略
propose / recommend / suggest a strategy	提議策略
adapt / change / improve / review / revise a strategy	修改策略
base a strategy on sth	把策略建立在～基礎上
underpin a strategy	支持、鞏固策略

strategy + V.

strategy be based on sth	策略建立在～基礎上
strategy be aimed at sth / be designed to do sth	策略目的在～
strategy depend on sth / hinge on sth / rely on sth	策略取決於～

strategy work 策略奏效

strategy backfire / fail 策略失敗

例句❶ The project is designed to help <u>formulate an effective strategy</u> for the promotion of internet connectivity in communities in southern Africa.
這項計畫目的在於，幫忙制定一個有效的策略來提升南非社區的網路連接。

例句❷ Concerns over the overuse of antibiotics have led to the need for <u>alternative</u> disease control <u>strategies</u>.
擔心抗生素被過度使用，這使得不同的疾病控管策略顯得必要。

例句❸ Changing the appearance of a well-known product can be a <u>risky strategy</u>.
改變知名產品的外觀可能會是個危險的策略。

例句❹ The charity is <u>mapping out a strategy</u> to meet the basic needs of the homeless.
這個慈善團體正在想辦法滿足遊民的基本需求。

例句❺ Instead of exploiting the poor, we have <u>developed strategies</u> to address poverty.
我們沒有剝削窮人，反而已經想出了解決貧困的對策。

例句❻ The teacher <u>employed strategies</u> to establish herself as the dominant voice in the classroom.
這位老師運用策略來使自己成為教室裡的主導者。

例句❼ <u>The strategy is aimed at</u> reducing the risk of accidents.
這個策略的目的在降低意外發生的風險。

A
B
C
D
E
F
G
H
I
J
K
L
M
N
O
P
Q
R
S
T
U

Talent 天資、天賦、天才　　　▶ MP3-235

Adj. + talent

extraordinary / formidable / incredible / prodigious / remarkable talent	非凡的、傑出的天賦
considerable / immense / tremendous talent	極大的天賦
genuine / undoubted talent	真的、不容置疑的天賦
exceptional / rare / unique talent	特殊的、少見的天賦
God-given / innate / natural talent	與生俱來的天賦
hidden / undiscovered talent	潛在的、未發掘的天賦
precocious talent	早成的天才
home-grown / local talent	本地的、本國的人才

V. + talent

possess a talent	擁有天賦
cultivate / develop / foster / nurture a talent	發展天賦、培養才能
harness / utilize a talent	利用天賦
put a talent to use	利用天賦
tap into a talent	挖掘並利用天賦、人才
discover / recognize / spot a talent	發現、發掘天賦
demonstrate / display / reveal / show a talent	展現天賦

| squander / waste a talent | 浪費天賦 |
| attract / bring in a talent | 吸引人才 |

talent + V.

| talent come from | 天賦來自於～ |

▶ MP3-236

例句❶ Whatever kind of writer you want to be, we'll help you tap into your hidden talents.
無論你想成為哪一種作家，我們都會幫助你發掘潛在的才能。

例句❷ Her talent was soon spotted and she made her stage debut aged 10.
她的天賦很快就被看見，10 歲時就首次登臺表演。

例句❸ At our school he showed talent as an actor in the drama group.
在學校時，他展現了身為一位劇團演員的天份。

例句❹ There is a wealth of talent out there in Hollywood Studios.
好萊塢有大量的人才。

實用短語 / 用法 / 句型

• talent pool 人才庫

• talent agent / scout 星探、球探、挖掘人才的人

• a wealth of talent 大量的、豐富的人才

• lend talent to （後面接公司、或是某案件）為～效力

Understanding 了解、理解力、同情心、協議

▶ MP3-237

Adj. + understanding

accurate / clear / complete / full / proper / solid / sound / thorough understanding	完全的、徹底的了解
basic / fundamental understanding	基本的了解
limited / rudimentary / superficial understanding	有限的、粗淺的了解
deep / detailed / in-depth / keen / profound / sophisticated understanding	深刻的了解
broad / comprehensive understanding	廣泛的了解
adequate / sufficient understanding	充分的了解
growing understanding	越來越多的了解
incomplete / poor understanding	了解不多
common / shared understanding	共同理解、同情
mutual understanding	相互理解
implicit / tacit / unspoken understanding	默契

V. + understanding

achieve / acquire / arrive at / gain / obtain understanding	得到對～的了解
broaden / build / deepen / develop / enhance / expand / extend / improve / increase understanding	加深對～的了解
advance / foster / further / promote understanding	促進、提升對～的了解
demonstrate / reflect / reveal / show understanding	展現、顯示對～的了解
call for / require understanding	需要對～的了解
assess / test understanding	評估對～的了解
seek understanding	尋求對～的理解
achieve / acquire / come to / form / gain / obtain / reach an understanding	達成協議

例句❶ The authority had a clear understanding of their operational policies.

政府當局清楚了解他們的經營策略。

例句❷ You need to read more extensively to gain a deeper understanding of the issue.

你需要更廣泛閱讀來更了解這個議題。

例句❸ The main objective of the event is to promote a better understanding of science.

活動的主要目的是提升對科學更多的了解。

例句❹ This change of policy reflects a growing understanding of the extent of the problem.

這一政策的改變反映了民眾越來越了解問題嚴重的程度。

例句❺ How children change so quickly is beyond my understanding.

孩子怎麼轉變如此快速,快到超乎我所能理解。

實用短語 / 用法 / 句型

- a lack of understanding 缺乏理解
- beyond (one's) understanding 無法理解

國家圖書館出版品預行編目資料

搭配詞的力量Collocations：名詞篇　全新升級版 / 王梓沅著；
-- 修訂初版 -- 臺北市：瑞蘭國際, 2019.03
288面；14.8×21公分 --（外語達人系列；20）
ISBN：978-986-96580-3-4（平裝附光碟片）
1.英語 2.名詞

805.162　　　　　　　　　　　　　　　　107009907

外語達人系列 20

搭配詞的力量 Collocations 名詞篇 全新升級版

作者｜王梓沅‧作者助理｜胡嘉修‧責任編輯｜林珊玉、王愿琦、葉仲芸
校對｜王梓沅、胡嘉修、林珊玉、王愿琦、葉仲芸、鄧元婷

英語錄音｜Leah Christina Zimmermann
錄音室｜純粹錄音後製有限公司
封面設計｜蔡嘉恩‧版型設計｜劉麗雪‧內文排版｜余佳憓、陳如琪

董事長｜張暖彗‧社長兼總編輯｜王愿琦
編輯部
副總編輯｜葉仲芸‧副主編｜潘治婷‧文字編輯｜林珊玉、鄧元婷
特約文字編輯｜楊嘉怡
設計部主任｜余佳憓‧美術編輯｜陳如琪
業務部
副理｜楊米琪‧組長｜林湲洵‧專員｜張毓庭

法律顧問｜海灣國際法律事務所　呂錦峯律師

出版社｜瑞蘭國際有限公司‧地址｜台北市大安區安和路一段104號7樓之1
電話｜(02)2700-4625‧傳真｜(02)2700-4622‧訂購專線｜(02)2700-4625
劃撥帳號｜19914152 瑞蘭國際有限公司‧瑞蘭國際網路書城｜www.genki-japan.com.tw

總經銷｜聯合發行股份有限公司‧電話｜(02)2917-8022、2917-8042
傳真｜(02)2915-6275、2915-7212‧印刷｜科億印刷股份有限公司
出版日期｜2019年03月初版1刷‧定價｜420元‧ISBN｜978-986-96580-3-4

瑞蘭國際